the bridesmaid

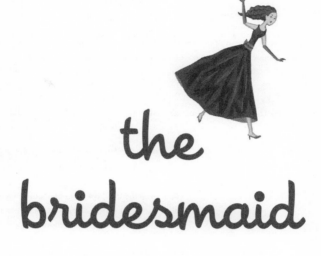

the
bridesmaid

hailey abbott

delacorte press

Published by
Delacorte Press
an imprint of
Random House Children's Books
a division of Random House, Inc.
New York

Produced by Alloy Entertainment
151 West 26th Street
New York, New York 10001

Visit us on the Web! www.randomhouse.com/teens
Educators and librarians, for a variety of teaching tools, visit us at
www.randomhouse.com/teachers

Library of Congress Cataloging-in-Publication Data is available upon request.

ISBN:0-385-73220-1 (trade)
0-385-90249-2 (lib. bdg.)

The text of this book is set in 11.5-point Baskerville BE Regular.

Book design by Angela Carlino

Printed in the United States of America

May 2005

10 9 8 7 6 5 4 3 2 1

BVG

Mr. and Mrs. David Beaumont

Request the honor of your presence

At the total disillusionment of their daughter

Abigail Lynn

Beginning June fifteenth

At the Dove's Roost Chateau

Watertown, Massachusetts

And lasting until Abigail's sister, Carol, gets married

Or Abigail loses her mind

Whichever comes first

Please use the enclosed R S V P

Prologue

This is the story of a girl who believed in love—love at first sight and love that lasted until the end of time. She believed every person in the world had one person they were meant to be with forever and always. She even thought that maybe, one day, she would find the very person meant for her.

But there was one tradition of love that Abigail Lynn Beaumont could never get into . . .

Weddings.

Abby was surrounded by evidence that love could last. Her parents, David and Phoebe Beaumont. Happily married family friends. And her favorite tried-and-true couple, Kermit the

Frog and Miss Piggy. (Although that one, she knew, was iffy, she really hoped those crazy Muppets could make it work.)

But our heroine was also surrounded by evidence that weddings were the source of all evil. Her parents were the proprietors of the Dove's Roost Chateau, one of suburban Boston's most popular catering halls. There, young men and women came together to vow to love one another forever and ever. And there, mothers of the bride threw hissy fits over flower arrangements; fathers of the groom shook their groove thangs on the dance floor until their pants rode down. Grandmothers and great-aunts and first cousins once removed drank exceptionally large amounts of pink champagne and went onstage to deliver very, very embarrassing speeches. But none of them, not the mothers or the fathers or the grooms or the maids of honor or even the little flower girls, were half as bad as the brides.

Brides.

Before she had even graduated from kindergarten, Abby had seen a bride slam a door in her father's face for suggesting that his daughter might want to powder her nose before the pictures. She had seen a bride reduce her mother to tears over the positioning of napkin rings. She had seen a bride throw a vase at her soon-to-be husband because he messed up her makeup when he kissed her. Abby couldn't stand brides. She couldn't stand the way they acted like the world revolved around them. She couldn't stand the way they'd be smiling sweetly and preening for pictures and then seconds later be screaming at a waiter about the temperature of the mini-quiches. She couldn't stand the way all of them, all of them, seemed completely awful. But since it was unlikely that all of these brides were just naturally terrible people, Abby knew

4

that meant only one thing—weddings turned ordinary women into Bridezillas.

Abby is, at this very moment, attending one of these infamously awful weddings with her older sister, Carol. We join her on a cool evening in the autumn of her seventh year. . . .

• • •

Abby and Carol Beaumont scurried under the gift table in the main dining room of the Dove's Roost Chateau catering hall, otherwise known as their home-sweet-home, and peeked out from under the white linen tablecloth. That night's wedding was in the process of unraveling and Abby's heart pounded in anticipation.

Already a big man had gone up to a skinny, dorky man and ripped off his bow tie. And the bride's mother had stormed out.

Abby watched her father get in front of the big man in an attempt to stop him from rushing the smaller man, who was red and sweaty and waving his arms like a cartoon character.

"What's going on?" Abby asked her sister, Carol. Carol was six years older and pretty much knew everything.

"The fat guy is mad at the skinny guy because the skinny guy won't pay for all the liquor the fat guy's family is drinking," Carol said sagely.

"How do you know?" Abby asked.

The bride was now crying in the corner.

"I listened."

Suddenly the fat guy reached past Abby's dad and grabbed a delicate china plate. Both Mom's and Dad's eyes widened as he pulled his arm back. Abby's dad made a last-second grab, but it was too late. The plate sailed by the skinny man's head and smashed against the far wall.

Why do they always throw plates? Abby wondered. *And why do they always miss?*

"Time to go," Carol said, taking her hand.

"No! I wanna see this!" Abby begged. She pressed her fingertips into the glossy wood floor.

"You know the rule. If dishes start to fly, we're supposed to go."

Carol dragged Abby, fingers squeaking on the floor, out from under the table. Another dish crashed, and together they ran outside just as the bride screamed, directly into her new husband's face, "He's *ruining* my wedding!"

The sun was setting, and a stiff wind blew dried leaves across the freshly mowed lawn. This was Abby's favorite time of year. Not only had soccer season just started up again, but also colder weather equaled fewer weddings. Fewer crazy strangers wandering in and out of her house, fewer creepy band guys grinning in her face and asking if she liked Mariah Carey songs, fewer crying brides with eye makeup streaked down to their chins looking like scary fancy-dressed clowns.

When they finally reached the little clearing in the woods behind the yard, Carol stopped pulling and turned toward Abby. She looked her straight in the eye and put her hands on her hips like she always did when she was about to say something serious.

"Let's swear we'll never get married."

"Never?" Abby squeaked.

"Never," Carol said. "If we ever do find our Prince Charmings, we'll just stay boyfriend/girlfriend and spare everyone the drama."

"So no stupid speeches and no big scary dress and no flying plates?" Abby asked.

"Exactly," Carol said. "Do we have a deal?"

"Yes."

Carol held her hand over her heart. "Okay, repeat after me. I, Carol Marie Beaumont, do solemnly swear that I will never get married and turn into a Bridezilla."

"I, Abigail Lynn Beaumont, do solemnly swear that I will never get married and turn into a Bridezilla," Abby repeated, copying Carol's pose.

Carol reached for Abby's small hands. "Now, remember what I told you about a promise made to a sister. . . ."

"I remember," Abby said. "A promise made to a sister is the most sacred promise there is on earth."

· 1 ·

Something Old, Something New

$\mathcal{A}$bby Beaumont was slumped in a chair in her mother's office, trying not to look out the window. The sky was blue, the sun was bright. It was absolutely perfect soccer weather. She would have given anything to be outside chasing the ball around, but instead here she was in her mother's froufrou office. Trapped.

On one side of the desk was today's VIC (Vomit-Inducing Couple), Kirsten and Brock, looking very pleased with themselves in matching polo shirts. On the other side was Abby's mom, dressed in a taupe-colored suit. Her slim fingers were a blur as she excitedly described the menu options at the Dove's Roost.

". . . and let's not forget about stuffed mushrooms, now those are really a crowd pleaser." Abby stared at her mother's Ace-bandaged right wrist, trying to heal the sprain with the power of her mind. She'd been trying all day. So far, no luck.

It was thanks to that wrist that Abby was stuck here in her mother's office—a room she usually avoided for fear of being sucked into a Laura Ashley vortex from which she might never return. The previous weekend her mom had insisted on wrapping the bougainvillea vine around the chuppah herself instead of waiting for Abby's dad to get home from Dell's Wholesale Liquor Mart like Abby had suggested. Her father was nearly tall enough to do it without a step stool and loved taking care of the outdoor work. But her mother had wanted to get a head start, had told Abby to hold the ladder, had climbed up it and had then promptly fallen from the top rung while trying to reach the edge of the canopy. Abby appreciated her mother's need to give her job 150 percent at all times, and she was glad the injury hadn't been worse, but now she was being robbed of a perfect-for-soccer Saturday. It was just wrong.

"And then, we want our first dance to be . . ." Kirsten stuck out one perfectly French-manicured hand like a stop sign. "'Lady in Red!'" She reached over and clasped her fiancé's fingers, the Rock of Gibraltar on her left hand flashing in the sunlight and blinding everyone in the room.

"Even though she won't be wearing red that night," Brock said with a grin.

"Of course not, silly." Kirsten smacked his beefy shoulder with her free hand.

"We danced to it the night we first met," Brock went on.

"I *was* wearing red *that* night."

"And I know you won't believe this, but, you know how at the very end of the song? You know how he whispers 'I love you' really softly?" Brock leaned in toward Abby's mother's desk like he was about to share a prized secret. Abby's mother was riveted. "Well, I swear I knew I was in love with Kirsten right at that very moment."

"And I knew I loved him too." Kirsten's grip on his hand tightened.

"*Oh!* That's so *sweet*," Abby's mother said with a wide smile.

Stewardess, I'll take that barf bag now. It was exactly this type of story that had inspired Carol to come up with the term VIC a few years ago. All the couples that came through the Dove's Roost seemed to have one of these sugarcoated cheese bombs to drop and they all felt the need to share them. Repeatedly.

"Abby? Did you get that?" her mother asked, turning in her big leather chair. "'Lady in Red' for the opening dance. We'll need to tell the band."

"Oh, I got it," Abby said with a tight smile, gripping her pen. "Lovely choice."

"Well, thank you!" Kirsten said. "You are so sweet

to help out your mother like this." She looked like she was about to burst into tears, that's how touched she was.

"Just happy to do my part," Abby said with a big toothy grin. When no one was looking she glanced at her watch.

Right about then she should have been down at Van Merck Park with Christopher and the rest of the soccer crew. If she were she'd be tearing down the sidelines, dodging and weaving, showing off the dexterous dribbling skills she had been working on all week long. But instead, she was stuck here, waiting for Kirsten's inevitable morph.

So far Kirsten, while far too chipper for this early in the morning, had shown no signs of scales or a giant green tail. But that would all change soon. Something would make her snap. Something *always* made the brides snap.

"Oh! And I've decided I want the Hearts Entwined ice sculptures," Kirsten said. "One for each of the stations at cocktail hour."

"A fine choice," Abby's mother said.

Abby made a note. Hearts Entwined ice sculptures at four stations. *One thousand dollars for frozen water. That's responsible spending.*

"Ice sculptures?" Brock said. "Um, honey, I thought we decided not to go with ice sculptures."

"No, Brock. Your father offered to put in more money, remember?" Kirsten said slowly. "That means we *can* have the ice sculptures."

Brock laughed nervously. Abby found herself inching to the front of her seat. This was it.

"I thought that money would be better spent if we put it toward our honeymoon," Brock said. "We've maxed out the Visa as it is. . . ."

"So? We have three more," Kirsten said.

"Do you really want to start our lives together that far in debt?"

"Do you really want to have cocktail hour tables with no centerpieces?" Kirsten asked, her grip visibly tightening on his hand.

"I'm sure there's something else we can do with the tables," Brock said, looking to Abby's mother for backup. "Phoebe? What do you think?"

"Oh, well, we can do some lovely things with the florist," Abby's mother replied brightly. "Or we can arrange the chafing dishes and platters in such a way that you won't need decoration at all."

Brock nodded. "That sounds good, doesn't it?" He looked relieved.

"No decoration on the station tables?" Kirsten said. Her mouth hung open in stunned horror. She shook her head slowly and narrowed her eyes. "Are you insane? Do you want me to have a substandard wedding?"

"No, honey—"

"Don't honey me! Lizzy Markowitz had ice sculptures at her cocktail hour!" Kirsten said, her face paling. "I *need* ice sculptures."

"Just because Lizzy had them? You hate Lizzy!"

"That's *why* I have to have them!" Kirsten stood

up. "My God, Brock! You don't understand me at all!"

"It's just frozen water!" Brock exploded.

"Thank you!" Abby blurted out.

"Abby!" her mother said through her teeth.

Kirsten couldn't have looked more offended if Abby had just suggested virginal white was not exactly her color. She burst into tears and ran from the office. Brock apologized and quickly followed. Abby leaned back in her chair with a sigh. She uncapped the pen again and wrote in her notebook.

Brock: 1

Bridezilla: 0

• • •

"Abby! How could you say that?" her mother asked as Brock and Kirsten stormed out the front door onto the lawn.

"What?" Abby asked, trying to look innocent. "I was just agreeing with the groom. I thought the customer was always right."

"Abigail Lynn, I know that sitting in on these meetings is not your idea of a good time, so I appreciate your offering to help," her mother said. "But I would appreciate it even more if you wouldn't antagonize the clients."

"Sorry, Mom."

Her mother went after Brock and Bridezilla and Abby headed for the foyer so she could watch from the front windows. Then Abby's father appeared from around the side of the house where he'd been assembling the lattice arch for that evening's ceremony.

He gave them a questioning look and then said something, which Abby knew was probably "What seems to be the problem here, folks?" because that's what he always said when something went wrong. He lifted his hand to his mouth and nodded in his concerned way as Kirsten did a dance of upsetness. Soon her father's hands were on both their shoulders and he was saying something. Kirsten's posture started to relax and Brock's face became a less disturbing shade of red. Crisis averted.

After a few more minutes Brock wrapped his thick arm around Kirsten's shoulder and they walked toward their silver BMW. Abby sighed and let the drape fall back down over the window. Her parents were so good at what they did. How they managed to genuinely care about each and every couple that came through the doors of the Dove's Roost, Abby would never understand. They were all so insipid, so spoiled, so obsessed with a ceremony that didn't actually *mean* anything. And yet, as far as Abby could tell, they spent so little time thinking about the eternal love that the ceremony was supposed to be about. All that mattered to them were color schemes, candle costs and whether to be announced as "Mr. and Mrs. Blabbedy Blah" or go the slightly more modern "For the first time as husband and wife, Blech and Blech Blabbedy Blah."

Abby was just about to run upstairs and grab her soccer ball when she heard squealing brakes on the back drive, accompanied by the telltale scream of an electric guitar. Abby smiled. Noah was here.

She walked back through the main hall and into the catering kitchen, where Rocco and Big Pete were busy assembling the chicken kiev for that evening's wedding. Little Pete—Big Pete's nephew—banged away at the back of the catering fridge. There was a loud slam, followed by a cry of pain.

"Oh, focaccia!" Little Pete came out from behind the fridge, a bandanna tied around his head, his thumb stuck in his mouth. He kicked the refrigerator door.

As always, the food smelled amazing. Abby grabbed a carrot stick and dipped it in Rocco's béarnaise sauce. There were a million drawbacks to living at the Dove's Roost, but at least the food was good.

"Abigail! That's for the guests!" Rocco scolded her with a smile.

"Put it on my tab!" Abby called.

Rocco and Big Pete laughed, their fast fingers never once pausing as they worked. Abby shoved open the back door just as Noah Spencer, bakery delivery boy extraordinaire, started up the steps. He was holding two pink boxes that almost jumped out of his hands when he saw her.

"You scared the crap outta me," he said.

"Just trying to help," Abby said with a smile and a shrug.

Her stomach was filled with that nervous-yet-pleasant tingling sensation she experienced every time she saw Noah. He was older, he was beautiful, and she'd had a crush on him since she was approximately nine and he'd saved her from a bunch of bullies on the playground at Van Merck. Noah had been riding his bike through the park, saw the fourth grade boys spinning Abby mercilessly on the merry-go-round and chased them off. From that moment on, Noah Spencer was her one and only, her dark-haired, blue-eyed knight in faded denim. But since he *was* older and beautiful and constantly treated her like a kid sister, she kept her crush to herself and did her best to treat him the way he wanted to be treated—like a big brother.

He walked by her and deposited the bakery boxes on the wooden pastry table.

"P.S., your pants are falling down," Abby said.

Noah hiked up his khakis and grinned. "Lost a little weight, I think."

"How you do that while working in a bakery I will never understand." Abby crunched her carrot. Noah's blue shirt made his incredible eyes look even more incredible than usual. She tried not to stare.

"Can I make up a plate for you and your pa?" Rocco asked Noah.

"You know it, Rock," Noah said. "Dad would kill me if I came home empty-handed."

Rocco started loading up a plastic platter with food. Noah turned and opened up one of the pink boxes, lifting out an intricately decorated layer of the cake. The yellow icing was covered with a white basket-weave design so detailed she could see the striations in the "wicker."

"Wow," Abby said, leaning her elbows on the table and getting in close. "Your dad does some amazing stuff with icing. This rocks."

"Yeah?" Noah smiled proudly. "Well, I guess he's the number one wedding cake guy for a reason."

"What flavor is it?"

"Nothing you'd like." He lifted out the second layer. "Chocolate with dark cherry filling."

"Dark cherry? Blecch." Abby stuck out her tongue. "How could they do that to their guests?"

"I'm going to pretend you didn't just insult my bakery," Noah said. "Besides, I happen to love the dark cherry."

"That's cuz you're a freak," Abby replied.

"Speaking of freaks, how's Johnny Rockets?" Noah grinned.

Abby sat down hard on a stool and rolled her eyes. "His *name* is Christopher," she said. "God! One little Fourth of July mishap and you're cursed for life."

Last summer her friend Christopher had helped his father—a local sportscaster who was also one of Watertown's volunteer firemen—set off the Fourth of July fireworks . . . and had stolen a couple to use at his own private party later that night. Christopher had managed to take down one of the oldest ash trees in the village and burn off one of his eyebrows—which had since grown back, but a bit darker than the other. All the kids in town had been calling him Johnny Rockets ever since. No one knew how the nickname had started, but Abby had always suspected that Noah had somehow had a hand in it.

"Fine! So how's *Christopher*?" Noah asked as he began to carefully assemble the cake into tiers.

"He's fine! Sheesh! Why do you always ask me how Christopher is and you never ask me about Delila or Carol or—"

"How *is* Carol?" Noah interrupted.

"She's great. Amazing, actually," Abby said. "She graduated summa cum laude from Harvard, you know."

"You've only told me two hundred times," Noah joked. "You'd think you were her grandmother, not her sister."

"Hey, I'm just proud of her. Is that so wrong?" Abby said. Graduation weekend in Cambridge had been amazing—a famous politician spoke at Commencement, and the Beaumonts had had a blast, spending the weekend at a fancy Boston hotel. The only bummer was, Abby hadn't been able to spend much time with Carol herself. There were too many cousins and friends and roommates swarming around. "Anyway, she'll finally be home next week. And, instead of moving into Boston like we thought, she's staying here while she does her internship at the Conservation Commission."

Abby shoved herself off the stool again and looked out the back window. The mother of that evening's bride, Mrs. Wolf, was there, directing her father and the florist as they wrapped white organza along the chairs for the ceremony. The woman actually snapped her fingers at Abby's dad and ordered him to retie one of his bows.

"I need out of this nuptial nightmare," Abby said under her breath.

"What's stopping you?" Noah asked, stepping up behind her. He was so close it gave her chills.

"I kind of live here, genius," she said, looking at him over her shoulder.

There was a tiny cut on his jawline left over from his morning shave and his breath smelled sweet and spicy like cinnamon. He was so kissably close and yet completely unkissable. Abby took a couple of steps away, hoping to slow her pulse.

"But you don't have to work here," he pointed out. "My dad needs me at the bakery, but your parents run this place like a well-canola-oiled machine. So . . ."

Abby blinked. "Driving a van and carrying boxes are not exactly rare talents. Any minimum wage moron could do your job."

Abby bit her lip when she realized how mean she'd sounded. This was one of her special talents—picking on Noah when all she wanted to do was tell him how perfect he was.

"You really know how to make a guy feel special, Beaumont," Noah said. Cake assembled, he wiped his hands on his pants and grabbed a Jordan almond out of a big bowl on the counter. "But back to you. We all know you're going to end up with some big soccer scholarship in a couple of years. You might as well ease the 'rents into the idea of an empty Roost while you've got the chance. Just go get another job. What's stopping you?"

Noah had a point. Her parents really *didn't* need her around here, did they? Well, except for right now because her mom's arm was out of commission. But on a normal day Abby only helped out here and there, making favors, pouring champagne, putting out place cards. And her mom had just promoted waitress, college student and lifelong bride wannabe Becky Taylor to assistant events director. Abby probably wouldn't even be missed.

But what would I do? Abby wondered. *Where would I work if I could work anywhere I wanted?*

"Thanks, Rocco!" Noah grabbed the covered platter and pulled open the back door. "Catch you guys later! See ya, Ab."

"Yeah," Abby said, her brain and heart still racing. "See ya."

•   •   •

That night Abby stood in the corner of the ballroom in her standard black dress waiting for the cake-cutting ceremony to begin. To her right stood Becky, who was, as usual, taken in by the intense *meaning* of the moment—something that was completely lost on Abby. Sure, the hall was gorgeous, even Abby could admit that. The chandeliers were dimmed and the candles flickering, their light reflected in the sparkling crystal champagne glasses; every surface was covered in rose petals. It was lovely. But it didn't seem to be about love. Love was supposed to be something that existed between two people, alone. Not between two people, surrounded by two hundred other people they barely knew, with a huge spotlight trained on them while they ate butter-filled chicken.

How could anyone think this process was special

and meaningful after watching almost identical cere-monies take place every Friday, Saturday and Sun-day night?

"Oh, just look at them! Those two are so *cute*," Becky gushed. "Aren't they so cute?" Becky said that every time about every couple. But she always really meant it. Abby rolled her eyes.

This bride was of the ruffle variety—ruffled skirt, ruffled sleeves, lots and lots of veil. Her groom looked like a string bean standing next to her. Together they cut into the basket-weave cake and everyone ap-plauded and clinked champagne glasses. Then the couple smeared cake all over each other's faces. Abby grimaced. Dark cherry goop was everywhere.

"Yeah," she said. "Adorable."

Becky let out a little sniff and wiped a single tear off her flawless brown skin.

"Becky," Abby said under her breath. "You don't even *know* them."

But Becky didn't hear her; she was too busy being moved.

"What? Why are you looking at me like that?" Becky asked. "Oh, God! Is my mascara running?" She whipped a compact out of a hidden pocket in her dress to check.

"No. You're fine," Abby said. "I'm gonna go find my parents."

She was halfway across the room when she glimpsed them, silhouetted against the light from the hallway, stealing a smooch as the cake was wheeled away to be sliced. *That* was romance.

Abby paused and smiled. Her parents were the ones that were just *so cute*. And, being a non-hugging, non-smooching, non-emoting type herself, their mushiness was about the only mushiness in the universe that she could tolerate. Because she knew it wasn't fake, it wasn't forced, it wasn't just a pose for some picture. Unlike the rest of what went on at the Roost.

"All right, everybody!" Romeo Monroe, leader of the band Premonition, shouted into his microphone. "Time to hit the floor for a little Electriiiic . . . Sliiiiiiddde!"

Half the guests screeched and squealed in glee. Moment over. If Abby witnessed one more sorry display of disco mayhem she was going to lose it. Seriously.

"You can't see it! It's electric!" the band sang as a hundred rhythmless guests took to the dance floor and the chandeliers began to quake. That was Abby's cue.

She'd already reached her cheese limit for the evening, thank you very much. She slipped out the back door and headed around the side of the Dove's Roost to her family's private entrance to the residence. Abby seriously wished Carol were there to gawk with her.

Just one more week, Abby reminded herself. In one week Carol would be home from Harvard. And unlike last year when she'd taken right off again to go on a Habitat for Humanity mission, this year Carol was all hers. Thanks to that coveted internship, Carol was going to be around all summer. Abby couldn't wait.

· · ·

Abby raced upstairs to her room and hit her phone's speed-dial button for Carol. She knew there wasn't much chance of finding Carol in on a Saturday night, but it was worth a shot. At least once a month Abby called to share the latest episode of *Brides Gone Wild.* The answering machine picked up on the third ring.

"You've reached Carol and Tessa. Leave a message!"

"Hey, Carol. Just stuck in the depths of wedding hell and needed a hand out. You know the drill. Call me tomorrow and I'll describe the most hideous gown in the history of bridal couture. Love ya."

Abby hung up, dropped back on her bed and sighed. *One week,* she reminded herself. *One more week and she's back! The Beaumont sisters are going to have the best summer ever.*

· 2 ·

Speak Now or Forever Hold Your Peace

"Beaumont! Heads up!"

Abby turned around just in time to see a soccer ball hurtling toward her head. She reached up and grabbed it out of the air before it had a chance to smash her nose.

Christopher Marshall pushed through the bustling hallway. "You were supposed to head it back to me," he said. He took the ball and dropped it on the floor. Christopher was about a foot taller and a foot broader than everyone else in the hall, the only guy in the sophomore class who filled out his burgundy Lockport jacket the way it was supposed to be filled. He had a chiseled face, blond hair and blue eyes that had every girl in the place lusting after him.

Everyone except Abby, of course. To Abby he was just the kid from down the street who had wet his bed till he was ten and once broke his leg dock-jumping on his dirt bike. Totally unlustworthy. But fun to have around.

"It's too early in the morning for headers," Abby said with a smile. She crossed to the other side of the hall. "Pass it."

Christopher tapped the ball toward her with his foot. A couple of freshmen jumped out of the way. Christopher jogged a few steps ahead and Abby passed it back, expertly avoiding a pack of gossiping seniors. She grinned and ran up. If only school could be all soccer, all the time.

"You missed an awesome scrimmage on Saturday, yo," Christopher said, passing the ball back.

Abby stopped it with her foot. "You think I *like* missing scrimmages so that I can sit home and help the mother of the bride reapply her mascara? Not likely."

She turned into their communication technology classroom. Her best friend, Delila, was already waiting for them at the table in the back. Christopher popped the ball up and followed Abby inside.

"Do you really have to do their makeup, yo?"

"Yo, Soccerboy, yo, you're not a rapper, yo, and you have to stop saying yo, yo," Delila said.

"Freakazoid," Christopher muttered with a sneer as Abby sat down between them.

Delila reached to turn on her computer. Her jacket opened slightly and Abby got a peek at the T-shirt underneath. "What is that?" Abby asked, pulling Delila's lapel aside. She was wearing a black concert T-shirt with a bright yellow-and-blue swirl design across the front. "Very non-reg." The uniform at Lockport was a burgundy jacket or sweater over a white shirt, black pants or a black skirt and black shoes, but Delila was always bucking the system. The Lockport faculty had long since given up commenting on Delila's red Converse sneakers or the fact that Delila almost never wore a white shirt. Somehow Delila Barber managed to be the constant exception to the rules. "I haven't taken it off since Saturday night," Delila said, her brown eyes bright. "You should've come, Ab. The concert was hot."

"Like I would really give up an evening of quintessential eighties rock and seventies dance tunes at the Roost to have an actual musical experience."

"Who'd you see, man?" Christopher asked.

"We're talking here, *man*," Delila shot back.

"Did you forget your Midol again?" Christopher asked.

"Okay, kids! Separate corners!" Abby said, lifting her hands.

For as long as she could remember, Abby had been mediating between her two best friends, but things had gotten even more dicey lately. Maybe it was a spring fever thing.

"So, did you ask your parents about Italy yet?" Delila asked.

The bell rang and Mr. Cox entered the classroom. As always, he immediately went to the board to write down that day's assignment, shattering chalk all over the place. Mr. Cox was a violent writer and a heavy typist, and he stomped through the halls like Frankenstein's monster.

"No, and I'm not going to ask them," Abby whispered. "When are you going to accept that I am not coming to Italy with you next year?"

"Oh, I don't know," Delila said with a smile. "Never?"

Abby sighed. Delila had been accepted into Lockport's junior year abroad program and was going to be spending months bopping around Italy from Venice to Florence to Rome—all without Abby. The very thought of spending an entire year at Lockport without Delila was horrifying. Abby would have loved nothing more than to go right along with her, but it just wasn't possible. Abby was already on partial scholarship at this savings-account-sucking school.

She just wished Delila would stop mentioning it all the time. Abby knew her friend meant well, but it was starting to upset her more than having to hear "The Bride Cuts the Cake" every weekend. (And that song could get stuck in a person's head for *hours*.) Thanks to the Italy trip, Abby was going to be on her own for junior year. Didn't Delila realize she was abandoning her best friend?

"Come on, Ab—"

"Look, there's no way my parents can afford to send me to Italy for an entire year." Abby kept her eyes straight ahead on the board, feigning attention. "You know I would kill to go with you, but it's just not gonna happen."

"Don't worry," Christopher said to Delila. "I'll be there to keep you company."

Abby's jaw dropped slightly. "*You're* going?" The only way she'd been able to comfort herself about Delila's upcoming disappearance had been the promise of a year of nonstop soccer with Christopher. It was the one thing keeping her from totally freaking out. Abby's heart started pounding in her ears.

"Got my acceptance letter Saturday," Christopher said. "*Buon giorno,* baby!"

"Oh no." Delila grasped both of Abby's wrists. "Ab, now you have to come. You have to be my testosterone buffer."

Abby let out a strained laugh and logged on to her computer. "Sorry, guys," she said, trying to force herself to sound normal. "Just try not to kill each other over there."

She clicked open the Internet browser, swallowing the lump in her throat. Christopher was deserting her too?

"You know, Beaumont, I wouldn't say no so fast," Christopher said. "Not until you have all the information."

Christopher reached into his backpack and pulled out a glossy book. He folded back the cover and placed it on top of her keyboard. Abby blinked. In front of her was the smiling face of Roberto Viola, the most famous soccer player in the entire world. Well, the most famous *retired* soccer player in the entire world. Below his headshot was a picture of him playing with two guys and a girl about her age, sweat flying everywhere.

"What's this?" Abby asked, picking up the book.

"That's the brochure for the Academy." Christopher was grinning widely. "Roberto Viola is the soccer coach."

"Shut *up!*" Abby whacked Christopher in the arm.

"Miss Beaumont? Would you mind keeping it down back there?" Mr. Cox was sitting at the front of the classroom behind the current issue of *Wired.* He didn't even look up.

Abby leaned in toward Christopher. "You're telling me that you are going to get to play soccer with Roberto Viola. Mr. Three Gold Medals, Mr. Four World Cups?" she whispered.

"Yep. I plan to come back for senior year a soccer God, yo." Christopher smiled proudly and leaned back in his chair.

"Wait a minute. You mean all I had to do all this time was show you that?" Delila pointed one orange-nailed finger at the page. "I've had that catalog for months."

"I guess you just don't know her as well as I do, yo," Christopher said.

"How about you get to know my foot, yo?" Delila shook her Converse in the air.

"Bring it on," Christopher shot back.

"I don't believe this," Abby said under her breath.

Suddenly it was all too clear. She'd worshiped Robert Viola since she was in third grade, when he scored the only two goals in the World Cup championship match. And now she might have the chance to not only meet him, but train with him?

"I have to apply," Abby said, half-dazed.

"Did she just say what I think she just said?" Delila turned toward Christopher.

"I think she did," Christopher replied.

They both sat forward and leaned in toward Abby. "You're gonna come?"

Abby looked at the smiling faces of her two best friends and felt her heart beat even faster. "If I get in and if we find a way for me to pay for it." Abby swallowed hard. She wanted this so much it was making her dizzy.

"Perfect! Check it out!" Delila gestured toward the board. "Today's assignment is 'Search the Web for scholarship options for Abby Beaumont.'"

"Actually," Abby said, reading Mr. Cox's insane scrawl, "it's 'Search the Web for online college courses and submit a list of twenty programs with their URLs. Mark down any navigation problems you see and how to correct—'"

"Why don't you get on that, Soccerboy?" Delila interrupted. "And make sure you get a couple extras so our lists aren't all exactly the same."

Christopher clucked his tongue and reluctantly got to work as Abby and Delila started their own Web search. Abby could barely contain her glee. If only this could work out, if only she could pull it off . . . next year could be the best year of her life.

And the first one that was wedding free.

Abby drove along the tree-lined streets of Watertown smiling. It was later that afternoon. Green leaves fluttered in the breeze, casting dancing shadows on the sidewalks and brick-faced buildings of Main Street. A couple of moms ushered their skipping daughters, tutus and all, into Marie's School of Dance. A pack of boys on dirt bikes pedaled by her at a stop sign and headed down the path toward Van Merck Park. It was all very suburban, very quaint, very spring, and Abby loved it. Living in a suburb so close to Boston gave her the best of both worlds—a laid-back town where people knew one another's names and were actually civil to one another, plus easy driving distance to Red Sox games, Revolution games and the Harvard campus where her sister resided. And today she loved her little town more than usual. Because not only was it a perfectly gorgeous spring day, she also had the inklings of a plan—a viable plan to flee the Roost.

Abby parked her white van in the strip mall parking lot in front of Spencer's Bakery, got out and slammed the door as hard as she could. The van had been around since Abby was a toddler and slamming was a necessity if she wanted the door to stay shut. At one point it had been the Dove's Roost equipment van—the vehicle her father used to run around town and pick up supplies and decorations. When Carol got her license, her dad had painted over the old Dove's Roost logo—two doves holding a string of wedding bells with their beaks—and given the behemoth

31

to the girls. The thing was unreliable and unsightly, but at least Abby had wheels.

The door bells tinkled as Abby walked into the window-fronted bakery, but no one came to the counter. The shop was empty. Abby inhaled that particular Spencer's Bakery smell, the combination of hot bread, butter, sugar and freshly brewed coffee that always made her feel both cozy and hungry. She'd been coming to this bakery for so long it felt like home.

There was music coming from the back room. She ducked behind the counter and strolled into the bakery kitchen. What she saw there made her slap her hand over her mouth to keep from laughing. Noah, with a smudged apron over his clothes and flour all over his face, stood in the center of the kitchen, playing air guitar along to the classic rock station on the radio. His eyes were squeezed shut in concentration.

Could he *be* any cuter?

"And you play your game!" he sang at the top of his lungs, the other bakery workers looking on and laughing. *"You give lo-o-ove a bad name!"*

Noah opened his eyes, spotted her and froze. Abby walked forward into the room, clapping. Noah's face flushed scarlet under the flour.

"Wow. You really missed your calling," Abby said. "That was cover-band gold. And trust me, I know cover bands."

"Nice to tell me we had company," Noah scolded his coworkers.

"Hey, Abby," a couple of the bakers greeted her before getting back to work.

"Hey, guys," Abby replied.

Noah walked over to the desk in the corner where he usually sat when he was taking orders or keeping the books. He dropped into his seat and started tapping on the computer as if he'd just been in the middle of something very important.

"What can I do ya for?" he asked, wiping his face with the back of his sleeve. Abby pulled a folded sheet of paper out of her jacket pocket. "Last-minute change for the Stewart wedding." She handed over her mom's scrawled note. "Thought I'd drop it off personally, but I didn't know I was going to be treated to a rock show."

Noah laughed and looked down at the note. "Tell your mom I'm on it."

"Okay! Catch ya later!" Abby turned to walk out. There was a freshly iced batch of cupcakes sitting on the counter and she grabbed one on her way.

"Hey! Those are for a birthday party!" Noah shouted after her.

"Good thing I know you always make extra!"

She walked outside and bit into the cupcake, smothering her lips with pink icing. There was nothing better than a postschool sugar fix. Not to mention a little postschool Noah fix. She was going to have the image of his air guitar solo burned into her brain for the rest of the week.

Abby finished up her snack, tossed the wrapper in a garbage can and was about to get back in the van when something caught her eye. In the window of Sports Expert, the mom-and-pop sporting goods store a couple of doors down from the bakery, was a Help Wanted sign. A Help Wanted sign in the window of one of her favorite stores on earth. *You can't do this,* Abby thought, her hand on the van's door handle. *Mom and Dad will kill you.*

But somehow that thought didn't stop her from walking into the store and grabbing the sign out of the window. This was her shot. She was never going to escape the Dove's Roost unless she started taking control.

Barb Miller's face brightened when she saw Abby come in. "Abby! What can I do for you today? We just got in a shipment of the new Adidas shorts. . . ."

"Sounds great," Abby said. "But first, let's see what I can do for you."

She placed the Help Wanted sign down on the counter and looked up at Barb hopefully. Sixty years old and she still ran the Boston Marathon every year. She had sold Abby her very first pair of shin guards back in the day. This woman was her hero. "You want the job?" Barb asked, her eyes crinkling at the corners. "Seriously?"

"Seriously," Abby said. "I'll fill out an application, I'll give you references. Whatever you need."

"No application necessary," Barb said with a smile. She tossed the Help Wanted sign in the trash can behind the counter. "You're hired."

• • •

That evening Abby sat at the table in the catering kitchen with her mother and father, putting together the favors for that Saturday's wedding. This week's bride had wanted to donate money to her favorite charity in lieu of favors, while her groom's mom had insisted that her friends deserved to go home with some little goody in their hands. In the end the family had ordered two hundred silver heart frames and now Abby and her parents were stuck placing cards into each of them that read, "A donation has been made in your name to the Free Cable Society." Abby's mom was cutting the cards into heart shapes using a template she'd made from the frame glass, her dad was using an eyeglass screwdriver to unscrew the tiny latch that held the backs of the frames in place, and Abby was removing all the paper inside, replacing it with the cards, then screwing the frames together again. They were going to do this two hundred times in a row.

Two. Hundred. Times.

"What's the Free Cable Society, anyway?" Abby asked.

"Damned if I know," her father replied. "People for gratis HBO?"

"Free cable car service in San Francisco?" her mom put in.

"Or maybe they want liberation for all the cable-knit sweaters of the world," her father continued.

Both Abby's parents laughed.

"Okay, you guys scare me," she said.

"I bet not as much as the thought of thousands of sweaters roaming free and wild!"

Abby smiled and struggled to slip the frame-back

into the little slot cut in the metal. She was too nervous to get her fingers to work properly. She had already put off telling her parents about her new job all afternoon and through dinner. Do-or-die time was rapidly approaching.

Abby's mother's cell phone rang—a tinny version of "Here Comes the Bride"—and her mother picked up the flip phone to check the caller ID. She groaned and tossed the phone into a box full of grosgrain ribbon, where it rang six more times before going silent. Abby and her dad exchanged a look.

"Sorry," her mother said. "It's just that Wentworth woman is getting on my last nerve. I think she may be a contender."

"For Most Horrendous MOB?" Abby's father sounded intrigued. "*Real*-ly?"

While Abby always found the Bridezillas to be the most obnoxious people in the wedding process, Abby's parents had a thing about mothers of the brides. They kept a running list of the most evil. It had been a while since they'd had a real possibility for the number one slot.

"She can't be worse than Mrs. Rosen," Abby said. "We had to redo her seating arrangement thirty-eight times. Thirty-eight!"

"I know," her mother said with a sigh, picking up the scissors again. "But I logged the number of minutes I spent on the phone discussing cake toppers with this woman. Anyone want to hazard a guess?"

"Half an hour?" Abby's father asked.

"Higher," her mother said.

"An hour?" Abby asked, incredulous.

"Two hours and forty-seven minutes," her mother said flatly. "Should they be crystal or ceramic? Modern or traditional? Do we know any good wood-carvers? Last night I spent half an hour explaining that unless she wanted to spend a thousand dollars on the cake topper, that no, there was no way I could commission someone to make one in the exact likenesses of the bride and groom."

"Is that how much it would cost?" Abby asked.

"I have no idea! I only said it in a vain attempt to make her hear herself," her mother replied. "But the joke's on me. She's actually considering it. Now I may have to find an ar*tiste* to do the job."

"Wow," Abby's father said. "I think we have a contender."

Her parents laughed and her dad put his hand over her mom's. They looked at each other and shook their heads, baffled.

"Just when we think we've heard it all . . . ," her mother began.

"There's always a real original waiting in the wings," her father finished.

Abby smiled. She loved how her parents were always finishing each other's sentences and how they took everything in stride.

At least they're in a good mood, she thought as they got back to work on the favors. *Just do it. Just . . . get it out there. Maybe it won't be as bad as you think.*

"So . . . guys. There's something I want to tell you," Abby said finally, laying her latest frame aside.

"This sounds serious," her father said jokingly.

"It is. Kind of. Well, not really," she added. Maybe it'd be best to act like this was no big deal. "It's just that I got a job today. That's all."

There was a prolonged moment of agonizing silence.

"You did *what*?" her mother demanded.

"You already have a job," her father said. "Here."

"Actually, I was thinking about cutting down on my Dove's Roost hours." Abby bit her lip. "Like maybe cutting them out entirely."

Her mother stared at her in disbelief. "Abby! It's spring!" she screeched.

"What are you thinking?" her father demanded, pushing his chair back from the table. "Do you have any idea how many weddings we have coming up?"

"Yes, Dad, I know. I know exactly how many weddings we have coming up," Abby said, reddening. "Don't you guys even want to know what the job is?"

"Oh, yes. Please tell us what could be so important that you'd leave your family in the lurch like this," her father said with uncharacteristic sarcasm.

"It's at Sports Expert," Abby said quietly. "Barb Miller hired me."

Her mother shook her head angrily. "Sports Expert? Of course. Better to stock tennis shoes than to help out with the family business."

Abby stared at her parents, suddenly feeling totally guilty. She hated hurting them, but she also hated how they just assumed she would be there. How they just expected her to be the good little wedding soldier when they knew she totally hated weddings.

Sooner or later her parents were going to have to realize that their kids had no interest in taffeta and tulle or the differences between white, ivory and bone.

"This is unacceptable, Abby. To go out behind our backs and get a job, without even asking us . . . this isn't like you," her father said.

"Dad, I'm sorry I didn't tell you beforehand, but it was a spur-of-the-moment thing. I just saw the sign in the window today. And besides, this way I'll be making extra cash," Abby added, trying to appeal to their logical sides. "I won't have to hit you up for new soccer cleats or gas money or . . . anything else. It'll be good for everyone."

"But Abby—"

"And you guys just promoted Becky! That girl would sell her Prada on eBay if it meant she could get more hours." She looked from her mother to her father and back again, her eyes begging. "Please, you guys? I really want to do this."

Abby's mother and father exchanged a long look and finally, her dad sighed. He picked up another frame and went to work on it with the screwdriver.

"Well, I guess we can't keep you prisoner here . . . ," he said. "So if it means that much to you . . ."

"Yes!" Abby said, jumping up and wrapping her arms around her father's neck. "Thank you! Thank you! Thank you!"

She kissed her dad on the cheek, then sat down

again, her fingers a lot less shaky. A tiny little part of her knew she should mention the Italy program, but after their drastic reaction to a mere job she decided to wait a bit. There was no telling whether she'd even get in. So there was no reason to rock the boat further.

Not yet.

· 3 ·

With This Ring

The front door flew open and Carol came tearing out.

"Ab!" Carol cried. "Abolina!" It was Friday after school and Abby had just gotten home.

"Carol!" Abby shouted. "You're home!" The sisters threw their arms around each other and hugged tight. "I thought you weren't getting here till tomorrow!"

"I decided to forgo the last night of post-graduation partying," Carol said. She lifted the soft auburn curls around Abby's face and let them drop back down against her cheeks. "God, why did you get the good hair?"

Carol's own straight brown locks were tied back in a loose ponytail, random pieces hanging carelessly around her face. She wore a purple T-shirt, beaten-up green cargo pants and Birkenstocks, her wrist-cuff tattoo and a slim silver ring her only accessories. She looked stunningly beautiful, as always.

"So how long have you been here?" Abby asked as they linked arms and walked up the front steps.

"A few hours. Mom is already trying to rope me into manning the ice cream buffet this weekend. What is *wrong* with people, Abby. Don't they know ice cream buffets belong at birthday parties for seven-year-olds?"

Abby laughed. Her sister had always been a dessert snob.

"I'm so glad you're here," Abby said. "Finally it's back to the way it should be. Us against them for the entire summer!"

"Well, Ab, actually there's something I want to talk to you about." They entered the foyer and Carol twirled around to face her sister. Carol's eyes were sparkling and she had a huge crazy-looking grin on her face.

"You're all hyper," Abby said. "What's your deal?"

"You'll see!" Carol said. She pushed open the door to the catering kitchen.

Their parents were already there, sampling Rocco's latest pasta concoction.

"Good! Abby's home!" their father said, rubbing his hands together. "We finally get to hear the big news."

"She's been practically bursting at the seams all afternoon," said their mother.

Abby looked at Carol's face and then was suddenly struck with a feeling. A very bad feeling. "Oh, God. You're not, like, going to the Congo for the summer with Greenpeace or something, are you?"

"No, nothing like that," Carol said, clasping her fingers together. "I'm getting *married*!"

Carol lifted up her hand and turned the silver band on her finger around, revealing a big, square diamond. Abby felt the earth tilt beneath her and she gripped the brushed-steel countertop for balance.

This was *not* possible.

"You're what?" Abby's mother was the first to find her tongue.

"To who?" Abby blurted out. She felt dizzy and her heart was pounding, like maybe she was about to pass out.

"To Tucker, Abby," Carol said. "Duh!" She rolled her eyes and then grinned. "Isn't it amazing? He asked me last night, but I wanted to tell you guys in person."

Wait a minute, Tucker Robb? Abby thought, reeling. Carol had only been dating Tucker for two months! And didn't the guy live in Colorado most of the year?

"Carol, we haven't even met this boy," their father said, looking confused. "You only just received your diploma."

"You would have met him, Dad," Carol said, sighing. "He still can't believe he had to miss my graduation, but his grandfather's health came first." Apparently Tucker's grandfather had emergency heart surgery in Ohio the day Carol graduated. "But you'll meet him soon. And he's not a boy. He's twenty-six. And if I remember correctly, you and Mom were married right after college."

"Yes, but we'd known each other for years," Abby's mother said. "Are you sure you're not rushing this?"

"You know me," Carol said confidently. "I wouldn't be doing this if I didn't know it was right."

There was a moment of silence as Abby's parents exchanged a look. Abby waited for one of them to say something. For them to let Carol have it. For them to forbid her to make this huge mistake, which was exactly what this was. A huge, *huge* mistake. Well, if no one was going to say anything, then Abby was. "But–but–Tucker lives on a ranch, Carol! A ranch! And you're–you're a vegetarian!"

But Carol just laughed. "Be happy for me," Carol said, stepping toward her parents. "Think about it. You get to plan my wedding! We're thinking August. And we want to have it right here, at the Dove's Roost."

"What?" Abby screeched. She looked over at her parents and realized they actually looked okay with this. They even looked like they were getting a little *excited* at the idea of planning Carol's nuptials.

Carol couldn't. She . . . she wouldn't. A Dove's Roost Bridezilla? It went against everything they had ever believed. It went against every fiber of Carol's being.

"But—but August is the hottest month of the year," Abby said, unable to come up with anything else.

"Abby," Carol said, approaching her with a smile. She reached out and took Abby's trembling hands. "You have to be my maid of honor."

"Me?"

Carol hugged her. "Who else would it be? Isn't this great?"

Abby stepped away from her sister, her mind reeling. There were so many things wrong with this whole situation, she could barely put them in comprehensible order.

"No! It's not great! What are you thinking?" Abby exploded. "You've only known this guy for, like, five seconds! And Dad's right! We've never even met him! And P.S., he lives halfway across the country! What're you gonna do, move to Colorado to tend cattle or something? What about your job?"

Carol's face dropped. "Actually, I've already declined my internship so I can concentrate on planning the wedding. But after the summer, yeah. We'll probably live out there."

"You declined your internship?" Abby stared at her sister. "Carol, you've been wanting that job since freshman year. You beat out a hundred other applicants to get it."

"I know, but I'll get another job in Colorado," Carol replied with a shrug. "They have a ton of great organizations out there. . . ."

Abby had the sudden gut-wrenching sensation that she didn't even know the person standing in front of her. Everything Carol was, everything she had always stood for, had been tossed aside. The job she always wanted? Who cared? The fact that she loved Watertown and Boston? Whatever. The independent, free-spirited, willing-to-jet-off-to-anywhere-at-a-moment's-notice girl? Gone forever.

"We haven't figured it all out yet, but I think what matters is that Tucker and I love each other and we want to be together," Carol said.

"So be together. You don't have to get married for that," Abby said. "What about the pact?"

The moment Abby said those words out loud she realized she sounded even more ridiculous than she already had. After all, as she'd grown older she had realized that the pact they had made as little girls might not hold up over time. But it was still the first thing that came to mind. Carol was deserting her for a guy Abby had never even laid eyes on.

It was supposed to be the two of them, the sane Beaumont sisters, versus the wedding insanity perpetuated by their nuptial-obsessed parents.

"Abby, now calm down," her father said. "It's good to voice your concerns, but if this is what your sister wants—"

"Come on, Dad. You were concerned two seconds ago," Abby said. "Up until you realized this gave you another wedding to plan."

"Now, Abby, that's unfair," her mother said.

"Maybe it is, but not as unfair as the fact that Carol's leaving us for some guy she hasn't even bothered to bring home. Doesn't anyone see that but me?"

"Look, I know it's kind of sudden," her sister said. "But I thought you'd be happy for me."

"Well, I'm not," Abby said, tears springing to her eyes. "I'm sorry, but I'm not."

She turned on her heel and ran for the stairs to the residence, taking them two at a time. There was no way this was happening. Just no way. Carol couldn't do this. She couldn't give up everything for some guy she barely knew. She couldn't desert Abby to go spend the summer at a slaughterhouse two thousand miles away. And if she thought Abby was going to stand up there and be her maid of honor while she made the worst mistake of her life, she had another think coming.

Abby slammed the door to her room, picked up her soccer ball and hurled it against the wall. It ricocheted off and took out an entire shelf of trophies. She flopped down on her unmade bed, curled into a ball and pulled the blanket over her head, the way she used to do back when she was a little girl. Back when Carol was still Carol instead of someone's wife-to-be.

•   •   •

When the knock came at her door fifteen minutes later, Abby half wanted to ignore it, but it wasn't like her entire family didn't know where she was. She sighed and sat up.

"Yeah."

The door opened and Carol walked in. Abby pushed herself back on her bed and grabbed a pillow, hugging it to her.

"Here to tell me the particular shade of pink I have to wear?" she asked.

"Abby, please don't tell me this is really about the pact," her sister said. "I mean, you didn't really still think we were never going to get married."

"No," Abby said. "But do you have to do it now?" *I thought I was getting you back, at least for a little while. And now you're leaving me—again.*

"Abby, listen, I know this is all out of nowhere," Carol said, sitting on the edge of the bed. She leaned forward and rested her elbows on her knees. "Trust me, I know. It was all out of nowhere for me, too. But when Tucker asked . . . it just felt right. I just knew." She paused and turned her ring between her thumb and forefinger. "It's hard to explain."

"But Carol, you're barely out of college," Abby said, pushing her hands into her bedspread. "You're gonna meet, like, a million more guys."

Carol laughed and turned her head to look at Abby. "Yeah, but none of them are gonna be like Tucker."

Abby's heart thumped extra hard. There was something about the look on her sister's face. Something had changed. Her sister had always been tough, headstrong and defensive most of the time. The girl had had political beliefs since the age of nine. Growing up, everyone had picked on her for being a vegetarian and for holding sit-ins in the cafeteria and boycotting Burger King. As a result of all this, Carol had always carried herself like she was ready for a fight, ready for someone to challenge her and ready to take the challenge.

But now . . . now it was like all the tension was smoothed out of her face. Like the defiance in her eyes had softened a bit. Like she wasn't so angry anymore.

"What?" Carol said. "Why are you looking at me like that?"

"I don't know," Abby said slowly. She suddenly felt uncomfortable. "You look different, I guess."

Carol's grin widened, lighting up the entire room. "I'm happy."

Abby looked down at her bedspread and sighed.

"Come on, Ab. You're gonna love Tucker, I swear," she added.

How am I supposed to love the guy who's stealing my sister? Abby thought.

Carol pulled her legs up onto the bed so she could face Abby. "This isn't a bad thing. It's a good thing," she said. "A really, really good thing."

Abby took a deep breath. And looked into Carol's face. Carol was staring back at her and she looked so happy, and so hopeful. "Please just be happy for me?" she asked. "Please?" And she smiled so sweetly. What was Abby supposed to do?

Abby sighed again.

"Well," Abby said slowly. "I would just like to mention ahead of time that I am *not* wearing poofs, bows or flower patterns of any kind." She tried to force her face into a smile, but a half-smile was all she could muster.

"You can wear whatever you want," Carol said. "And I promise you won't have to do anything but show up."

"Swear?" Abby asked.

"Swear," her sister said. "I know how you feel about weddings, Abby. I'm not gonna be a Bridezilla, I promise."

"Carol, it's inevitable. No one is immune. We've seen it happen a zillion times."

"Exactly! That's what gives me the edge." Carol shook her finger at Abby. "I can fight it because I know the signs. I'm not going to let the curse of the Dove's Roost get to me. No siree. And besides, it might be nice to get all dressed up and party with the people we love."

Abby took a deep breath. "Okay," she said. "Okay."

Carol leaned over and hugged her tightly. "It really means a lot to me that you're okay with this."

But I'm so not, Abby thought, her heart full as she hugged her back. *I'm so not okay with any of this.*

• • •

An hour later, Abby was doing what she did best—taking her frustration out on the soccer field. She dribbled along the sideline, breathing in bursts, her pulse pumping in her ears. She saw Rob Rand coming at her from the corner of her eye, straight across the field. He didn't think she saw him coming, so she let him believe she was oblivious. She kept dribbling and running until the very last second. Rob made a play for the ball but it was no longer there—Abby had passed it cross-field to Christopher. And Rob ended up right on his ass.

Normally, in a pickup game such as this, Abby might have taken a split second to gloat, but she couldn't stop. She was in the zone. And as long as she was in the zone, she wasn't thinking about anything else. Weddings, sisters, Bridezillas. None of it existed in the zone.

Keep it . . . Keep it . . . , she thought as a couple of defenders came at Christopher. She ran to center field and Christopher popped the ball perfectly to her. Abby stopped the pass and turned. Everyone had been covering Christopher. It was all open field between her and the net. Britney Cox was in goal. Please. Abby could beat that little frosh any day of the week.

Abby raced up, faked left, and as soon as Britney dove for the phantom shot, Abby kicked hard and put the ball right into the top left corner of the net. Abby felt the familiar little rush of happiness that always followed a goal.

"Whoooo!" Christopher shouted, running toward her.

Abby let Christopher sweep her up into a sweaty hug, then she slapped hands with the rest of her makeshift team. This was another fabulous thing about living in Watertown. Both Lockport Academy and Watertown High had been turning out state champion soccer teams for as long as the town could remember. There were so many soccer players and wannabes walking around, finding a game was never a problem. And after the big announcement, there was nothing Abby needed more than a game.

"Want a ride home?" Christopher asked, heading for the sidelines.

"Wait, what?" Abby replied, sucking wind. "Aren't we still playing?"

"We were playing to five," Christopher said. He pointed over his shoulder at the goal. "That was five."

"Really?"

Abby checked her Nike watch and sighed. It was already six o'clock. Where had the time gone?

"Actually, I think I'm gonna jog home," she said. "Do a little cooldown."

And maybe take the longest available route, she added silently. On the way to the field, Abby had used every shortcut, wanting nothing more than to get out there and kick the ball as hard as possible, as often as possible. But now she was thinking about running down by the water and back up through Main Street to get home. . . .

"Avoiding your sister, huh?" Christopher said, grabbing a towel to swab his face. "I can't believe she's getting married, yo."

"Join the club," Abby said.

"Do you think she'll, like, have kids right away? That'd be insane," Christopher said. "You'd be Auntie Abby."

Kids? Abby hadn't even thought about kids. But that was what married people did, right? Procreated?

"I've got to get out of here," Abby said. "See ya."

Before Christopher even had a chance to utter a goodbye, Abby was tearing across the field. It was amazing. The day before Abby couldn't wait for Carol to get home. And now all she could think about was avoiding her.

ENGAGEMENTS

Phoebe and David Beaumont, residents of Watertown, announce the engagement of their daughter Carol Marie to Tucker Robb, son of Clint and Mary Robb and stepson of Sharon Robb, all of Denver.

The bride-to-be is a recent summa cum laude graduate of Harvard University, where she majored in environmental science and public policy. She will not be immediately pursuing a career in this field, however, opting for a summer off to immerse herself in the Culture of the Bride and thereby shave at least fifty points off her IQ.

The groom-to-be is a graduate of the University of Colorado and has just received his EdM degree at Harvard. Strangely, all other pertinent facts about the groom are as yet unknown, even to the bride's family, who we'd think would at least be clued in to his middle name and medical history before Carol tied herself to him for all eternity.

An August wedding is planned, after which the couple will reside just outside Denver, which is exactly 1970.07 miles from Boston.

· 4 ·

Here Comes the Groom

$\mathcal{A}$bby sat in her room, trying to read the list of topics she had to study for her history final, but she couldn't concentrate. In ten minutes or less, Abby was going to meet the enemy. The guy who had lobotomized her sister. Tucker Robb.

It had been two weeks since her sister's big announcement, and the wedding planning was zooming at full-speed ahead. Amazingly the Dove's Roost had had a cancellation, and Mrs. Beaumont had immediately slotted Carol and Tucker's wedding into the available prime slot. Carol had already hired their parents' favorite band, Twilight, and secured a justice of the peace to do the ceremony. Her parents had even laid out deposits! And now Tucker was on his way to the Dove's Roost, where he was going to be staying for the next month—all the way up to the day of the wedding. Abby hated to admit it, but it looked as if this thing was actually going to happen.

Abby had been doing everything she could to think about the wedding as little as possible. And that meant being at home as little as possible. She'd picked up extra shifts at the store, spent hours at the library studying for finals and hid out at Delila's house whenever she could. Last Saturday afternoon while Carol and her parents had interviewed photographers, Abby had snuck over to her best friend's house, where Delila had spent three hours perfecting Abby's mother's signature, then forged it perfectly on the application for Student XChange. Once that and the financial aid package were sealed, Abby and Delila had kissed both envelopes and said a little prayer over Delila's mailbox before tossing them in.

Which meant Abby was doing two things— excitedly looking forward to getting the response to her application. And dreading the arrival of Tucker.

Suddenly Abby heard the crunch of the gravel at the bottom of the driveway. She looked out her window to find a black Ram pickup truck rolling toward the fountain that centered the circular drive. God! The guy even drove a gas-guzzler. Was Carol under some kind of mind control? The front door slammed and Carol flew over to the driver's-side door, yanking it open before the truck even stopped moving.

"Puke on a stick," Abby said under her breath.

Then came her very first view of Tucker Robb, the man who would be her brother-in-law. He stepped out of the truck and wrapped her sister up in a hug, taking her off her feet. He wore pressed khakis, a green plaid shirt and work boots. His blond hair was shaggy on top and short on the sides and from where Abby stood he appeared to have the chiseled features of a movie star. Not surprising. Carol had always dated pretty boys.

After a long kiss, Carol dragged Tucker inside by the hand and the door slammed again.

"Mom! Dad! Come meet your future son-in-law!" Carol called in a singsongy voice.

"Ugh. Puke on a stick with mustard," Abby said, slumping back in her chair.

Almost instantly the muffled, excited voices of her mother and father sounded from the foyer. She could hear Tucker's voice—a baritone—and his throaty laugh. In fact he was laughing *way* too much. Either he was nervous or a total suck-up. "Abby!" Carol shouted up the steps. "Tucker's here."

Abby forced herself off her bed. What exactly was the point of all this? There was no way she was ever gonna like the guy who was making her sister move clear across the country.

She clomped down the stairs, arms crossed over her chest, and stopped a few feet up from the happy family unit that was gathered below. Tucker looked up at her and smiled, flashing pearly whites.

Wow, he was *really* hot. There had to be something wrong with him.

"Hey, Ab," Tucker said. "It's nice to finally meet you. Carol talks about you 24/7."

"Hi," Abby said, walking down the last few stairs.

So here he was. This was him. The guy who was taking Carol off to live with five dozen future sides of beef in a state she'd never been to. Abby leaned her side into the banister and wondered how long she had to stand here before she could retreat to her room again.

She imagined Carol's voice inside her head. *You're being a brat,* she would say. Abby knew it was true, but she couldn't seem to make this heavy feeling in her chest go away.

"So . . . ," Abby said, feeling like she had to say something.

Suddenly Tucker grabbed her up in a tight bear hug. Abby let out a surprised squeak as he pinned her to him. Her lower arms flailed out at her sides helplessly.

Invasion of personal space! Abort! Abort!

"This is so cool! I've never had a kid sister!" Tucker said. He smelled all musky and guylike. Abby would know, what with her nose mashed against his shoulder.

"Can you let go of me now?" Abby asked.

Tucker relented and stepped back. "Sorry. Guess I got a little carried away."

A little? Abby thought, her face burning.

"We should have warned you, Tucker. Abby isn't the touchy-feely type," Abby's mother said, an amused smile playing about her lips.

"Oh, right," Tucker said with a laugh. "You did say that, Carol, huh? Sorry."

"You'll have to get used to Tucker hugs," Carol said, looping her arm through his. "He *is* part of the family now."

Abby swallowed hard. Now they were all looking at her with amused, patronizing smiles. She couldn't believe this. The four of them, standing there together, looking at her like she was the outsider and they were the family.

"So, I hear you're a talented little soccer player," Tucker said brightly, as if oblivious to her cold-as-ice body language. "We can kick the ball around later if you want. I could show you a few pointers. . . ."

Who said I need pointers? Abby fumed. And was it just her, or was he treating her like a five-year-old? Who did this guy think he was?

The guy who's marrying your sister, a little voice in her head warned her. *Chill before you say something stupid.*

"Tucker played for the Colorado soccer team," Carol said, casually resting her free hand on his chest.

Suddenly Abby felt even smaller and more childish than she did before. She'd never touched a guy like that. She couldn't even imagine feeling that comfortable around a guy. Well, except for Christopher and that was a just-a-friend kind of comfortable.

"Actually, I have to work this afternoon, so—"

"Really? What's the job?"

"She's working at a sporting goods store in town," her father said.

"Dad, I can talk, you know." Abby's face was burning.

A tense silence filled the room. Clearly she was bringing the happy-go-lucky, touchy-feely, hug-loving family down.

"So, Tucker, why don't you come inside? Have some coffee?" Abby's mother said, reaching for his arm. "I want to get to know the man who's swept my daughter off her feet."

"Sounds great," Tucker said, following her toward the kitchen. Abby's dad went with them. Carol turned around and shot Abby a wide-eyed look.

"What?" Abby mouthed.

"I knew you were going to do this," Carol said. "You decided not to like him before he ever even got here, didn't you?"

"I didn't have to!" Abby replied, even though it was true. "He was totally talking down to me. You were all treating me like I was a baby!"

"Well, if you're going to act like one . . . ," Carol said.

Abby narrowed her eyes, stung. "Thanks a lot."

Carol groaned and took off after the others. Abby hesitated a second, then stomped back upstairs. Luckily she had to get ready for work. Thank goodness Noah had given her the idea to come up with an escape plan. These days she needed an out more than ever.

• • •

"Abby, would you please help this customer with the cleats?" Barb called out. It was later that day. Abby climbed down from the step stool behind the counter. When she reached the ground she turned to find Christopher smiling down at her.

"Hey!" Abby tucked a stray curl behind her ear. Barb moved off to deal with a mom-and-daughter combo. "What are you doing here?" Abby whispered.

"Like she said, I need some cleats." Christopher headed for the wall of shoes. "Thought I'd throw my best friend some business. You gotta keep this job if you're gonna save up for Italy, yo."

"Well, thanks for your support," Abby replied. "What do you need?"

Christopher picked out a few pairs and Abby retrieved the shoes from the storage room. She dropped the boxes at his feet and sat down next to him on the vinyl-topped bench, happy to have the chance to take a load off.

"Aren't you gonna lace them up for me?" Christopher joked.

"Don't push it," Abby said.

Christopher extracted the first pair of cleats from the box and went about removing the inserts.

"So, how's everything with your sister, yo?"

"I met her man this morning," Abby said, pulling her knees up under her chin. "Can't stand him."

"What? Why?" Christopher asked.

"He totally talked down to me. He heard I was a 'good little soccer player,'" she said, putting on a doofy voice. "And he was acting like—I don't know—like he was already part of my family—looking at me like he knew *so* much about me." She glanced down at Christopher's feet and grimaced. "P.S., those are not attractive."

"They're not supposed to be attractive. They're supposed to be functional," Christopher said, getting up to give them a test walk. He paused in front of the mirror and looked down at the neon yellow and puke green cleats. "Whoa. Those *are* ugly. So, what else? I mean, is the guy cool on any level?"

"Well, he's pretty good-looking, but maybe too good-looking, you know?" Abby said.

"No. How can anyone be too good-looking?"

"It's not that, really," Abby said, struggling to put her feelings into words. "It was like he was too *on*. His hair was just the right way and his teeth were totally white and he was beyond polite and attentive to my mom. He had my parents laughing, like, all morning. I could hear them from my room."

"So what, he's a big suck-up or something?" Christopher asked. He dropped down next to her again and yanked off the cleats. "You think he's a fake?"

"It's hard to explain," Abby said. "I just get a bad vibe from him. Don't you get a vibe from some people?"

Just then, the door to the shop opened and Noah walked in. Abby's heart did a little flip, and then a flop. Noah was smiling until his eyes fell on Christopher and Abby.

"Whaddup, Johnny Rockets?" Noah said, lifting his chin in greeting.

Christopher gave Noah the up and down as he worked his foot into another shoe. "You're the cake boy, right?"

Noah let out a short exhale through his nose and then turned toward Abby. "I was just at your house and met your sister's fiancé?" He looked very confused.

"Oh, yeah. Carol's getting married," Abby said flatly. "Whoo-hoo."

"I can't believe you didn't tell me!" Noah said. "I mean, I've seen you five times since she apparently told you guys."

"Sorry," Abby said. "I guess I just assumed you'd already heard."

"Aren't you psyched?"

"Yeah," Abby said flatly. "Totally."

Abby got up and started pacing. Somehow she'd expected Noah to be as shocked and appalled as she'd been. She was expecting antiwedding solidarity.

"He seemed pretty cool," Noah said, walking over to her.

"I don't know . . . he's all right," she said unconvincingly. "Like I was just telling Christopher, he just seemed a little *too* perfect. Didn't you feel it when you met him?"

"Feel what?" Noah asked.

"A vibe. Like he's trying too hard," Abby said. "Like maybe he's trying to cover something up with all this forced perfection."

She looked up at Noah and he nodded knowingly, then shook his head at her. "What?" she asked. "What's that look?"

"Sounds to me like you're looking for reasons not to like the guy," Noah said.

"What's that supposed to mean?" Abby asked, her face growing red.

"That you don't want to like him, so you're coming up with reasons not to."

"Dude, what's your problem?" Christopher asked, looking from Abby's stricken face to Noah.

"No problem," Noah said. "I just . . . I suggest you jump on the bandwagon here, Ab. Your sister's gonna get married no matter how much you mope and pout and slam doors."

Abby felt the color rise in her cheeks. "I am not moping and pouting and slamming doors," she lied. How did he *know* that?

"Hey, I know how you feel about Carol," Noah said. "I'm surprised you've lasted through her entire college career. You can't stand it when she's away, so of course you're gonna hate the guy who's whisking her off to the Rockies."

"Oh, please." Abby felt her face getting even hotter.

"Come on, Abby, you know exactly what I'm talking about," Noah said with an amused smile. "Remember when she went away to summer camp when you were twelve and left you behind? You spent the first two weeks of the summer whining and sulking. And making the lives of everyone around you miserable."

"That was, like, sixth grade, yo," Christopher said.

"Well, she did it again when Carol was a freshman and every September since then," Noah said.

Oh, God! Noah *thinks I'm a baby?* Abby was mortified. *This day just keeps getting worse and worse.*

"So? So what if I love my sister?" Abby said. "What's wrong with that?"

"Nothing. It's great!" Noah said. "But it's also the point. This is your sister, Abby. It's *Carol.* Can't you just be happy for her?"

Christopher stood up next to Abby, squaring his shoulders like he was her personal security detail. "Look, man, Abby thinks the guy is fake," Christopher said. "And besides, Carol's freakin' twenty-two years old. Who gets married when they're twenty-two?"

"Come on, Ab, be honest," Noah said, looking Abby in the eye. "Did you even take the time to get to know the guy?"

Abby looked down at her feet. What was it with Noah today? It was like he'd developed psychic powers or something.

"Ever hear of gut instinct, yo?" Christopher asked.

"I'm trying to have a conversation with Abby," Noah said firmly.

"Well, from where I'm standing you're not even listening to her," Christopher replied.

"I don't really care how it sounds from where you're standing."

"Dude, you want to step off or what?" Christopher made a move toward Noah.

Noah didn't flinch and Abby suddenly realized things were about to get bad. What was wrong with boys anyway?

"You guys, chill out," Abby said, stepping up next to them. "God, you want me to lose my job?"

Christopher stared right past her at Noah. Abby gave Noah a pleading look, hoping to appeal to his more mature, less testosteroney nature.

"Fine, I'm going," Noah said. He looked at Abby and sighed. "Just think about what I said and try being happy for her. Hopefully this only happens once in a lifetime, right? You don't want to wake up one day and realize you screwed up your sister's wedding."

And without even looking at Christopher, Noah turned and walked out, leaving Abby with a fresh ball of guilt in her chest. She hadn't thought about it that way—that this was a once-in-a-lifetime deal. Maybe Noah was right. Maybe it was time for her to jump on the bandwagon. The problem was, her heart was much too heavy for her to feel like jumping.

"That guy's a jerk," Christopher said. "He's always had it in for me for some reason, yo." He blinked and looked at Abby, tipping his head to the side. "Hey. Maybe he likes you."

"What?" Abby blurted out, blushing. "Please. I don't think so."

"No no no. I'm serious. Think about it. I bet money he's jealous of me," Christopher said. "I speak for all guys when I say the whole best guy friend thing throws us off when it comes to girls. Seriously. Why else would he always be such a jerk to me?"

"Um, maybe because you're polar opposites?" Noah dated girls like Courtney Elefnate and Diana Waters—the two most beautiful girls at Watertown High. Girls with mystique and presence and two-hundred-dollar highlights. He would never like Abby—the girl whom he had called Ab*normal* for most of her formative years. The girl who, he'd said himself many times, was like the sister he'd never had.

"I'm gonna go put these in the back," Abby said, grabbing up the rejected cleats.

"Fine, don't believe me!" Christopher called after her. "But I'm right, yo! I have a sixth sense about this stuff!"

Abby ducked into the stockroom and leaned back against the wall to catch her breath, clutching the cleats to her chest. But that wasn't possible. *Was it?*

• • •

That evening Abby came home to the familiar sights of a wedding in progress. There were dozens of cars parked around the house and twinkling lights in the ballroom windows. Mike and Stephano, the valet guys, were sneaking cigarettes near the bushes by the kitchen. She nodded hello to them and headed in the side door. All she wanted was to get upstairs, take a long shower and call Delila. She had to talk to her friend about Christopher's theory. On something as crucial as this, Abby needed a second opinion.

As soon as Abby opened the door, she paused. Her parents' voices, tense and hushed, were coming from the residence kitchen. This was odd on two levels. First, her parents were never in the residence while there was a wedding going on. Second, her parents' voices were never tense, especially not when talking to each other. Abby approached the kitchen with caution. Her parents stopped talking the moment they saw her in the doorway. They were both dressed up in their wedding-night digs, and they both looked harried.

"Hey," Abby said, putting her bag down on a chair. "What's going on?"

"Nothing," her father said quickly. "How was work?"

"It was fine," Abby said. "What's the matter?"

Her mother exhaled loudly and smiled, running her hand over her forehead. "It's silly, really. Your father and I were just discussing themes for Carol's wedding. I want to do an English garden theme—"

"Which is overdone and completely passé," her father said.

Abby blinked. Okay, had he just interrupted her?

"And your father wants to do a candy store theme, which I think is far too cutesy and unsophisticated for Carol," her mother finished.

They both looked at Abby expectantly and Abby stared back until she realized they were expecting her to break the stalemate. This was too weird. "Why don't you just throw some flowers on the table and be done with it?" she suggested. "There's no reason to get all stressed about it. I mean, I'm sure Carol doesn't care."

From the looks on her parents' faces she may as well have just told them Carol was dead.

"What?" Abby said.

"How can you say that?" her mother asked. "Abigail Lynn, this is your sister's *wedding.*"

"Abby, your mother and I have been doing this for years, just looking forward to the days when we could use our expertise to plan your and your sister's weddings," her father said. "We are not going to just throw some flowers on the table and be done with it."

"I'd think you'd want better for your only sister," her mother put in.

Well, at least they're agreeing now, Abby thought. *Agreeing that I'm the party pooper.*

Abby heard Carol's quick and light steps on the stairs. She practically skipped into the room and over to the refrigerator.

"Hey, everyone!" she said, smiling as she popped open a Snapple. She whirled and looked at her family. "Whoa. Who died?"

Just then the door to the residence opened and closed and Tucker shuffled into the kitchen, looking down at a piece of lined paper. He stopped at the threshold, his brow furrowed, having yet to notice he had company.

"Good evening, Tucker," Abby's father said.

Tucker visibly started, folded the paper up and shoved it in his back pocket. The color rose in his cheeks and he smiled nervously. Abby felt her internal radar go off. Something was up.

"Baby!" Carol exclaimed, rushing over and planting a quick kiss on his lips. "How was the mall?"

"Uh . . . fine," Tucker said, shifting his weight from foot to foot.

"You let him brave the Plaza alone?" Abby's mother joked. "I'm surprised he found his way back." The Plaza mall was sprawling and crowded and notoriously void of parking.

"I know. I should've gone," Carol said, wrapping her arm around Tucker's waist. "But I wanted to get a jump on the Colorado job hunt. I spent half the day on the Internet."

Abby swallowed hard.

"What were you shopping for?" Abby's dad asked.

"I needed some . . . socks." Abby glanced at his hands. No sign of any bags. "They didn't have any," he added quickly.

"They didn't have any socks? At the mall?" Abby asked.

Tucker let out a laugh and backed out of the doorway. "Not the kind I wanted. Guess they only have them back home."

"Tucker's all OCD about certain things," Carol explained, grinning. "Socks being one of them." She reached out and grabbed his hand. "Are we still going to the wharf?"

"Yeah! Yes!" Tucker said quickly. "I'm gonna just go . . . change." He turned and jogged up the stairs.

Abby looked at Carol and her parents. They hadn't seemed to notice a thing.

"What's with him?" Abby asked.

"I think he's adjusting to the idea of being here," Carol said. "It can't be easy living with the future in-laws. Especially if they're giving you the third degree about socks," she added pointedly to Abby.

"What'd *I* do?" Abby asked.

"Nothing. Forget it," Carol said. "Do you have any plans tonight?"

"Well, I—"

"Because I thought you might want to come with us," Carol interjected. "You know, get to know him a little?"

Oh jeez. How am I gonna get out of this one? Abby thought. But one look at her sister's hopeful face, and she knew she wasn't going to say no. Clearly this meant a lot to Carol. Maybe Noah was right. Maybe it was about time Abby tried jumping on the band-wagon. And she could start by being nice to her future brother-in-law. Or trying to, anyway.

The thought of Noah made Abby remember how desperately she needed to call Delila to go over every-thing. But apparently that was going to have to wait.

"Okay," she heard herself say. "I'm in."

• • •

"Wow," Tucker said. "This is really beautiful." He, Abby and Carol were drinking lattes from Starbucks and walking the boardwalk down by the water. Though she didn't want to admit it, Abby had to agree with Tucker.

One side of the walk was lined with stores, every-thing from an old-fashioned cheese shop to a wooden toy maker to a Häagen-Dazs and a Gap. On the other side, small-craft docks jutted out into the water. There were lanterns strung from poles to light the way for nighttime boaters. The water lapped up against the pylons, making a soothing, sloshing sound. Abby took a deep breath of the evening air. She loved coming down here at night.

"It must have been so cool growing up here," Tucker added.

He reached out and entwined the fingers of his free hand with Carol's. They exchanged a private look. Abby turned her head.

"Yeah, we loved it," Abby said. "Carol especially. She used to visit every day to throw bread into the water and watch the fish come up for it. And then, of course, yell at all the fishermen."

Carol laughed as a breeze blew her hair back from her face. "Oh, God. I was so obnoxious."

"You *yelled* at the fishermen?" Tucker asked, grinning.

"I figured someone had to tell them what they were doing was murder," Carol replied with a shrug. "Might as well be me."

"What would your twelve-year-old self think if she knew you were marrying a *rancher*?" Abby joked.

The smiles slowly fell from their faces. Abby looked away again and sipped at her cardboard cup of coffee. He *was* a rancher, right? And Carol *was* a vegetarian and animal rights activist. She was just stating the obvious. And if stating the obvious made Carol wake up and realize she was making a mistake, then she was doing her sister a favor, right?

"Oh, hey," Carol said suddenly. "I'm gonna run into the bookshop and see if Raina's around. I haven't seen her since I've been home."

"Okay. We'll be out here," Tucker said.

Abby resisted the urge to chase after her sister shouting, "I know what you're up to!" It couldn't have been more obvious that she was leaving her and Tucker alone on purpose. She and Raina Burton, whose family owned Burton Books, were only casual friends in high school. Carol normally wouldn't have gone out of her way to see the girl. Abby had been set up.

"So," Tucker said.

"So," Abby replied.

"Can we walk out to the end of one of the docks?"

"Sure."

Together they clomped along the nearest dock, an uncomfortable silence hovering between them. When they got to the end, Tucker sat down and dangled his legs over the edge. Feeling awkward standing alone, Abby sat too.

"Listen, Abby, I know this whole thing's gotta be tough on you," Tucker began.

Oh, I so don't want to have this conversation, Abby thought.

"I mean, it's gotta be weird. Carol and I just met and maybe I'm not exactly the person you envisioned for her," he added. At that moment Abby realized she never had envisioned the guy Carol would end up with. Up until recently she'd never really thought past next week.

"We know what our obstacles are and we're working them out," Tucker continued. He looked Abby in the eye for the first time and hazarded a smile. "I guess I just hoped that you wouldn't be one of them."

Abby's stomach felt hot. There was nothing worse than being put on the spot.

"Carol loves you. You're pretty much the most important person in her life," Tucker continued. "I know it would mean a lot to her if we got along and it would mean a lot to me, too."

Abby looked down at the water, her eyes threatening tears. She had no idea what to say. If there was one thing Abby was bad at it was one-on-one, loaded conversations. She usually avoided them at all costs. But he did sound sincere.

Abby thought of Carol. She thought of how *she* might feel if Carol treated Noah like dirt. Then she just wanted to throw herself off the dock and drown. The last thing she wanted was to cause Carol pain. She loved her sister, and she knew Tucker was right—that Carol loved her, too.

"So? Whaddaya say?" Tucker asked.

"Well, if it really means that much to you. . . ," she said jokingly.

"Thanks." Tucker's face brightened. "I'm really not a bad guy. I swear."

"I guess you couldn't be," Abby said. "I mean, if Carol likes you. She has very discerning taste."

"That she does," Tucker said. "She thinks I'm OCD about socks? Would you believe it took her two hours to buy a pair of jeans the other day?"

"It usually takes me three," Abby confessed.

They both laughed and Abby looked down again, the unpleasant warmth fading and leaving a sort of reluctant tingle in its place. Maybe she could do this. Maybe Tucker wasn't so bad after all.

"It'll be nice to have an ally," Tucker said, lifting his coffee to his lips. "You're aware that your parents are one hen short of a henhouse, right?"

"Oh, I'm aware," Abby said. "Normally I'd tell you to run while you still could, but I don't think Carol would appreciate that, so all I can do is say . . . good luck."

She held out her hand to him and Tucker shook it with a smile. "Thanks," he said.

Abby grinned. "You're gonna need it."

Save the Date, Pardner!

We're gettin' hitched!

Carol Marie Beaumont has lassoed herself a groom in
Tucker Clint Robb.

The ceremony will take place August fifteenth
at the Dove's Roost Chateau
Watertown, Massachusetts
Be there or be hog-tied!

· 5 ·

Till Death Do Us Part

Abby padded downstairs in her oversized Lockport Academy T-shirt and went directly for the fridge. Her eyes at half-mast, she reached in for a can of pineapple chunks and her hand hit something gooey. Frowning, she pulled back her custard-covered fingers and looked inside the refrigerator. The entire second shelf was filled with desserts—chocolate mousse, raspberry tart, custard cups and strawberry trifle, among other things.

"What the . . . ?"

She shoved the trifle and custard aside and dug into the back for her smoothie ingredients. When she slammed the door a moment later, a note that had been taped to the fridge fluttered to the floor. Abby bent to pick it up with her free hand.

Carol—

Congratulations on your engagement!

May I suggest one of our signature desserts to complement your wedding cake? I'm leaving these samples with your parents, but we can make anything your imagination desires. Feel free to give me a call!

Sincerely,

Cheryl Martin

Delectable Desserts

Abby dropped the note on the counter. Unbelievable. If there was one rule her parents always adhered to it was that wedding business never invaded the residence. That was why they always worked on favors in the catering kitchen and had designated an office as the craft room downstairs. But apparently now that Carol was the bride, all rules were off.

Abby turned to dump her things on the counter, but it was covered with bridal magazines, their pages bookmarked with Post-it notes. Sighing, she used her elbow to shove them out of the way and knocked over an open box in the process. It hit the floor and little vials of confetti exploded from inside, showering the tile with silver wedding bells, pink hearts and white doves.

Abby groaned loudly, dropping the pineapple, the carton of yogurt and a tray of ice on the counter. She picked up the box and used her arm to swipe the confetti toward the side of the room. It was way too early to be breaking out the vacuum.

Taking a deep breath, she peeled a banana and then tossed it along with the rest of the ingredients into the blender. It wasn't until the grinding noise started to wake her up that she realized how quiet it was. Too quiet.

She stopped the blender, her hand still holding the lid down. Wasn't it Sunday? And if it was Sunday, wasn't it big breakfast day? So where exactly was the big breakfast?

Just then she heard the voices, heated and strained, coming from outside. They got closer and closer to the front door until it finally burst open and suddenly the room was full of noise. Her father, her mother, Carol and Tucker were all talking over one another as they entered the house.

Tucker placed a big brown bag of bagels on the counter and leaned toward Abby.

"You'll want to run," he said under his breath. "Now."

"What's going on?"

"Like I know? They've been arguing about color schemes for the last forty-five minutes," Tucker said. "Honest to God I've never even heard of some of the colors they've brought up. I mean, what's cerise?"

Abby was about to answer, but her mother's voice cut her off.

"Red? How can you even think about red, David? This is a summer wedding!" she cried.

"Red is her favorite color, Phoebe," her father replied, leaning back into the counter. "Isn't it, Carol?"

"Well, yeah, but—"

"What about an all-white wedding? If everything was just covered in white it would be just—"

"Boring. Just boring is what it would be."

"Like red is so original?"

"At least it has *something* to do with our daughter!"

Carol pushed her hair behind her ears and her ring twinkled in the sunlight streaming through the windows. Abby just could not get used to that rock. It seemed so out of place on her sister's finger.

"Do we really need a color scheme? Can't we just mix it up? Have it be sort of *au naturel*?" Carol said, looking innocently hopeful. Both her parents turned toward her.

"But, Carol! You have to have a color scheme!" they said in unison.

Ooookay. Time to bail, Abby thought as the argument escalated. She reached for a travel coffee mug, poured half the smoothie into it, and inched around the perimeter of the kitchen until she got to the stairs. Tucker shot her a helpless sort of smile.

"Sorry," Abby mouthed.

"Save yourself," he mouthed back.

Abby turned and bolted up to her room. Maybe Tucker wasn't so bad after all.

• • •

That afternoon Abby returned home from a long run to find a wedding in progress. The bride was just starting down the aisle in the backyard, so she slipped as quietly as she could through the side door, then headed up to her room to call Delila.

She was just sitting down with her cordless when Carol burst into her bedroom, the color high in her cheeks.

"Hey. Knock much?" Abby said.

"Sorry." Carol closed the door. "I need to talk to you."

Abby put the phone aside, intrigued. This was high intensity stuff, whatever it was.

"Abby, I have never seen Mom and Dad like this," Carol said. She pushed her hands through her hair as she paced the area rug in front of Abby's bed. "First it was color schemes, then they moved on to invitations and place cards and whether to invite Donny and Beth and if so, whether we should have an open bar. . . ."

Abby stifled a laugh. Donny and Beth were the raging alcoholics of the family who just *loved* to make a scene at any and all functions.

"It's not funny!" Carol said. "I'm telling you, you should have seen them! I think my wedding is going to kill their marriage."

Abby chewed on her lip. "Come on, Carol. Don't you think you're being just a little dramatic?"

"No! No I don't!" Carol sat down on the bed and pulled one leg up on top of the blankets, then started gnawing on her already gnawed fingernails.

"Okay, stop doing that before you draw blood," Abby said, putting her hand over her sister's.

"Sorry," Carol said. She pulled her angry, red pinky free and sucked on it. "You have to help me, Abby. You have to help me plan the wedding. If Mom and Dad do it, they're going to kill each other. I swear it's like this whole thing has set off some kind of latent power struggle between them. They're not themselves."

"Wait a minute, wait a minute, wait a minute," Abby said, pushing herself off her bed and backing up slightly. "You want me to *plan* your *wedding*?"

"Well, not the whole thing," Carol said. "I just need your help taking some of the responsibilities off Mom and Dad."

"But Carol . . . you said all I had to do was show up. I hate weddings. You know this."

"I know," Carol said. "Which is why *you* know I wouldn't ask unless I thought it was important. Abby . . . I just want to have a nice wedding. And it would be great if our parents made it through it in one piece."

Abby saw the sadness and hope in her sister's eyes and felt herself caving. The last thing she wanted in this world was to plan a wedding, let alone her sister's premature, ill-advised one. But how could she turn down a face like that from the person she loved most in the world?

She took a deep breath, closed her eyes and dove. "I'll do what I can."

"Oh! Thank you! Thank you, thank you, thank you!" Carol cried. She hugged Abby so tight, she could barely breathe.

"I wouldn't thank me yet," Abby said as she finally extricated herself from her sister's freakishly strong grip. "I'm sure I'm going to suck at this."

"Not possible," Carol said.

Abby couldn't help but smile at her sister's confidence. "Oh, and hey! I get to pick out my own maid of honor dress," she said.

"That's a given," Carol told her. "I promise."

She squeezed Abby's hand, gave her one last grin and walked out the door. From the yard Abby heard the string quartet break into the classic bridal recessional.

Abby wasn't sure whether to laugh or cry.

• • •

"Okay, the first thing I need you to do is come up with a song list," Carol told Abby. It was later that evening and the two sisters and Tucker were sitting under the stars in the backyard, kicked back on lawn chairs. Carol had a fat, spiral-bound book titled *The Ultimate Wedding Planner* on her lap. It was already jam-packed with budget lists, graphs and tear sheets from magazines.

"You guys don't want to do that yourselves?" Abby asked. "It's *your* wedding."

"Yeah, but beyond Sarah McLachlan and the Beatles, I'm musically challenged," Carol said.

"What about you?" Abby asked Tucker.

"I'm all about Tim McGraw," he said, arms crooked behind his head.

"Okay, I'm on the music!" Abby announced, widening her eyes. She uncapped the pen and got to work. "No 'Celebration,' no 'Hot, Hot, Hot.' No . . ."

"Put down songs they *can* play," Carol said with a laugh.

"Oh. Right," Abby said.

She glanced over at Noah's van, which was sitting in the delivery parking lot. He had gone inside fifteen minutes ago to collect the cake plates from that day's wedding and had yet to return. Her heart had been pounding ever since he'd shown up.

"I'm going to go make a phone call, sweetie," Tucker said, getting up and pulling out his cell phone.

"Who ya callin'?" Carol asked.

"Oh, just my dad. He left me a message earlier. Something about the tuxes," he said. "I'll be back in a sec."

As Tucker walked in through the back door, Noah came out. Abby suddenly felt like she was on the verge of collapse. Good thing she was already sitting.

"Hey," he said.

"Hey," she replied.

"Can I talk to you?" He tilted his head toward the van.

"Sure." Abby somehow squeezed the word through her windpipe.

This was her chance. She was going to study Noah for any and all signs of crushing.

Just keep it cool, she told herself, wiping her palm on her jeans. *Act normal.*

"So you decided to give this whole wedding thing a shot," Noah said as they walked. "I just wanted to say I think that's really cool."

"Thanks." Abby studied his eyes, looking for some sign of the feelings Christopher had mentioned.

Nothing.

"What's that?" Noah asked, glancing at the pad she still clutched in her hands.

"Oh, song list," Abby said. "I'm working on what *not* to play. I have many ideas on the subject."

Noah smiled. "Need any input?"

He didn't touch her or move closer to her or execute any of the acknowledged flirting techniques. He just stood there and looked at her. Abby tried not to drown in disappointment.

"Please. She's already sucked me into this nightmare," she said, finding her voice. "You should save yourself."

"And you should accept help when it's offered," Noah replied. "It's only gonna get crazier."

"Good point," Abby said, noting that his hair was mussed and his shirt was stained from the bakery. If a guy liked a girl, wouldn't he clean himself up before coming to her house? "Okay. You want to come up with the songs they're *allowed* to play? I can't seem to think of anything."

"Done," Noah said.

"Thanks. I'm feeling totally clueless," Abby said.

"Well, that's nothing new," Noah joked.

"Ha ha," Abby said, her face burning. Christopher was so off. These were not the words of a person in love. Or even in like.

"I'll e-mail you or something," Noah said, getting in the van.

"Cool," Abby said.

"Anything for you, Ab."

Abby sighed as Noah backed up and headed down the driveway. *Maybe Christopher is right.* A breeze lifted her hair off her neck and she shivered.

"Carol! I'm gonna go get a sweater!" she called out, glad for an excuse to be alone for a few seconds and refocus her brain.

"Okay!" Carol replied.

Abby jogged inside, down the hall to the residence and up the stairs. She was positively giddy.

Okay, calm down. Noah gives you one nonsarcastic remark and suddenly he's in love with you? Not likely, she told herself. *You're basing most of this on an observation by Christopher Marshall. This is the same person who thought* Frankenstein *was a true story.*

She was about to head into her room when a voice froze her in her tracks.

"No . . . no . . . you can't do this to me."

It was Tucker, but his voice was coming from the bathroom.

"No . . . Melissa . . . listen. I'm serious about this. . . ."

Abby turned her head toward the bathroom. *Melissa?* Blood started to pound through her veins.

There were a few more muffled words and Abby crept down the hallway to hear better.

"Melissa . . . please . . ."

Please? Please what? Abby thought. Was Tucker cheating on her sister right in her own house?

Her foot hit the floor and the board beneath her let out a loud creak. Abby flew into her bedroom across the hall and quietly closed the door. She held her breath as she heard the bathroom door open, saw the shaft of light in the crack between door and floor. Finally it closed again and the light was gone. She heard Tucker saying goodbye and then waited as he walked back downstairs. Only when she heard the door between the residence and the Dove's Roost close was Abby able to breathe again.

She walked shakily over to her bed and sat down. She knew it! She *knew* Tucker was too good to be true! *Oh, God. Why did I have to come upstairs?* Abby thought.

But then . . . wasn't it better this way? If she hadn't come upstairs just then, she never would have found out who this guy really was. Sure Carol would be crushed for a while, but that was infinitely preferable to hitching herself to a cheater, right?

Abby leaned back on her bed and went over everything she had just heard. She knew exactly what Noah would say. Maybe Tucker's actions were suspicious, but she hadn't actually heard anything that proved his guilt. He hadn't said "I love you" or "I need you" or "Meet me down at the docks for some mad, crazy sex."

I need more proof, Abby thought. *I just have to find out what he's up to for sure. Find out who Melissa is. And once I do, Carol will thank me. She'll thank me for stopping her before she makes a seriously huge mistake.*

Abby's list of songs NOT to play at the wedding:

"Celebration" (Come <u>on</u> already)

"We Are Family" (Enough. We know you got all your sisters. We're very happy for you. Move on.)

"Hot, Hot, Hot" (No one looks good doing the conga.)

"I Will Survive" (Why do they play this at every wedding? It's a breakup song. Are the bands trying to be ironic?)

All songs with accompanying choreographed dances, including, but not limited to:

"Macarena"

"Electric Slide"

"The Chicken Dance Song"

"Locomotion"

"The Twist"

Any and all love songs (Kind of hypocritical considering the groom may be fooling around on the bride, no?)

· 6 ·

Bridal Chic

*A*bby rested her forehead on the table and let out a groan. Delila looked up, her green eyes expectant beneath her battered Dave Matthews Band baseball cap. "*Come stai,* Abigail?" she asked.

"*Io,* um, *stai* bad," Abby said. It was Monday after school and the two friends were sitting outside at Starbucks.

"Okay, your Italian sucks donkey doody," Delila said.

"D, what am I gonna do?" Abby asked, sitting up. "Can I really let her marry this guy?"

Abby took a sip of the espresso Delila had ordered for her and almost choked. After consuming one quarter of the cup her entire mouth tasted like the drain in the bottom of the catering sink after a wedding.

"P.S., this stuff sucks," she said.

"You're gonna have to get used to it if you're going to Italy," Delila said. "When in Rome . . ."

"Okay, forget Italy," Abby said. "What do I do about Tucker?"

Delila leaned back in her chair, squinting toward the sun as if it held the answer.

"You really think he's cheating on her?" she asked.

"D, you should've heard that phone call," Abby said. She clasped her hands together dramatically. *"Melissa . . . please! You can't do this to me!"*

"See, that's what doesn't make sense," Delila said. "I mean, if Tucker's the one getting married then what is *Melissa* doing to *him*? If he's in a relationship with this girl and he's leaving her to marry Carol, wouldn't it be the other way around?"

Abby blinked. This was why she needed Delila around. The girl had a normal thought process instead of the knee-jerk reactions Abby normally relied on.

"I guess . . . ," she said slowly.

"Look, all I'm saying is give the guy a chance before you condemn him," Delila said. "From the physical description he sounds totally yum." She raised her eyebrows and slurped noisily at her coffee, then ran her tongue over her top lip.

"Gag!" Abby said with a laugh. "But I guess you're

right. Actually, Noah said the same thing to me the other day and I practically ripped him to shreds."

"Poor Noah," Delila said with a little pout. "Doesn't he know you need a good twenty-four hours before you can process anything rationally?" Abby sighed and looked out across Main Street as cars whizzed by, headed for baseball practices and Girl Scout meetings. Right about then Carol and Tucker were meeting with the justice of the peace, discussing their wedding ceremony. Abby felt a lump in her throat as she imagined her sister excitedly discussing vows and processionals.

"So, speaking of Noah . . . ," Delila said. "What was this you mentioned to me today about a possible reciprocation of your lifelong embarrassing crush?"

Abby sighed, wishing she could muster up some of the Noah enthusiasm she'd felt the day before. It was tough to switch gears from her sister's unfortunate situation to her potentially fortunate one. Abby felt guilty just for *thinking* about being lucky in love.

"Well, Christopher thinks Noah likes me," she said.

Delila's face fell. "*Christopher* thinks? There's a reliable source. Why don't you just call one of those midnight psychic nine hundred numbers?"

"Thanks for the support."

"Sorry. Hey, you know I think Noah's an idiot for not noticing your hotness long ago," Delila said. "If Christopher's right, I'll be the first one at the happy couple party."

"Thanks," Abby said, looking down.

"Hey? What's with the face?"

Abby shook her head and attempted to smile. "There's just so much going on. Between Tucker and all the wedding insanity . . . Did I mention my parents are staging a literal War of the Roses?" Abby said. "I've never seen them so riled up about flowers before."

"Come on. This is Dave and Phoebe we're talking about," Delila said with a grin. "They live for this. They must be so stoked now that it's Carol."

"I don't know," Abby said. "They don't usually interrupt each other and talk over each other like this. It's weird. I'm telling you, I don't even want to go home today."

"Well, my friend, it sounds like you need a vacation," she said, slapping her book down on the table. She looked at the cover picture of the Roman ruins as if she'd never seen it before. "I know!" Delila said, her face lighting up. "How about Italy!"

Abby laughed and pulled the book toward her. She scanned the photo of the crumbling Colosseum, the exotic-looking minicars, the European street signs. It was all so different, so exciting, so . . . not here. She hugged the book to herself and smiled.

"Just imagine. One year from now, we might be sipping *real* espressos at a real café," Abby said.

"And two hot Italian guys will stroll by and stop—dazzled by our beauty," Delila put in, sitting forward.

"And they'll tell us how *bella* we are and how they want to whisk us away to the Mediterranean Coast. . . ."

"So we'll hop on the back of their little motor-bikes . . ."

"And we'll speed off," Abby said, shaking her head back. "And I will be blissfully unaware of the latest trends in wedding gowns. . . ."

"And your guy . . . Sergio . . . a distant cousin of Noah's who actually notices perfection when he sees it . . . will ask you if you will agree to never, under any circumstances, marry him." Delila spread her hands wide in front of her as if painting the tableau before them.

"And then he'll take me to a professional soccer game," Abby stated. "Now *that* is romantic."

"It's perfecto!" Delila said. "Too bad Soccerboy's gonna be there to muck up the works."

"Delila, this anti-Christopher obsession has got to stop," Abby said.

"Look, all I'm saying is that with Soccerboy in Italy, Sergio may get the wrong idea." Delila took a sip of her coffee and looked away.

Abby watched her for a moment, confused, and then sat up straight. "Wait a minute, wait a minute. You don't think *Christopher* likes me, do you?"

"Well, you guys *are* always hanging out together," Delila said.

"We're friends! You know we're just friends," Abby said with a laugh. "God! Doesn't anybody think that guys and girls can just be friends anymore?"

Delila pressed her lips together and shook her head. "Nobody has ever thought that guys and girls could just be friends."

"Well, then we're the first of our kind," Abby said. She slumped back in her chair and crossed her arms over her chest. "Sheesh. I thought it was the twenty-first century. Besides, Delila, if Christopher liked me do you think he would be telling me he thinks *Noah* likes me?"

"Who knows why Soccerboy does the things he does?"

"D!"

"Okay, okay," Delila said, raising her hands. "You don't like Soccerboy and Soccerboy doesn't like you. Thank God. By the way, you've got a few doves and hearts dangling from your sleeve."

Abby lifted her arm and, sure enough, there were a dozen pieces of confetti stuck to the pilly weave of her Lockport sweater. How the heck had they gotten there? She groaned as she attempted to brush them off.

"Have I been walking around like that all day? When were you going to tell me?" she said, tossing the confetti at Delila's face.

"What? I thought it was a new look. Maid of honor chic."

Abby laughed and rolled her eyes. There was no denying it. This wedding was following her everywhere.

"I have an idea," Delila said. "I've got some Italian language tapes in the car and you don't want to go home. Want to go to Van Merck and practice?"

"Totally," Abby said.

"Good. Let's stop off at your place and get that old portable stereo of yours," Delila said.

"Okay, but doesn't that defeat the whole me-not-going-home scenario?"

"Please. We'll be in, we'll be out, the Bridezilla will never even know we were there," Delila said, gathering her things.

"I don't know," Abby said as she followed her friend toward the street. "They can smell fear."

• • •

"Let me just run upstairs and get some sunblock," Abby said. "You know me. It's never too early in the year to get freckles."

Abby opened her bedroom door and stopped so fast Delila rammed Abby's dad's ancient boom box right into Abby's back. Abby's normally messy bed was made and covered with bridal magazines, open and dog-eared with shoes and earrings circled in red and Post-its sticking out from various pages. On her dresser a wheel of fabric swatches was splayed out and three pictures of bridesmaids' dresses were propped up against the mirror. Her *Bend It Like Beckham* poster had been partially covered by a corkboard with to-do lists and business cards pinned all over it. Carol and Tucker were sharing Abby's one desk chair, all cuddled up against each other as Carol clicked the mouse on Abby's computer.

"Oh . . . my . . . God," Delila said, hugging the stereo to her chest with both hands. "It looks like a *girl's* room."

Carol and Tucker turned around and smiled. "Hey! Hi Delila! How've you been?" Carol asked.

"Fine!" Delila said with forced brightness. "Congrats on the whole wedding thing."

"Thanks! This is my fiancé, Tucker." Tucker stood.

"Nice to meet you," Tucker said, reaching out a hand.

Delila's eyes widened as she looked up at him. "Whoa," she said as they shook hands.

"Whoa what?" Tucker smiled.

"Uh . . . strong grip," Delila said. Then she turned to Abby and mouthed, *"He is hot!"*

Yeah. Hot and unfaithful, Abby thought.

"So, Abby, I hope you don't mind," Carol said, looking around. "If I keep all this stuff in my room I won't be able to *think* about anything else. I'm already driving myself crazy."

"So . . . what? Now I get to be crazy?" Abby dropped her bag in the small area of free space left on her bed. There was a pair of high heels circled on one of the closest pages–pointy-toed Dyeables with skinny little stilettos. "I hope you don't expect me to wear those," she said. "I'll kill myself." She lifted the photograph close to her face. "And most likely take someone with me."

"I haven't decided on anything yet," Carol said, beaming. "I'm still just getting ideas."

"Carol, you can't keep all of this in here." Abby tossed her sweater in the closet. "Seriously. It's too much."

"Come on, Ab. It's just a few magazines," Tucker

said. "We'll stack 'em up in the corner and you'll never notice."

"A few magazines and my computer, apparently," Abby said. She leaned in over her desk chair to see what her sister was looking at. There were thumbnails of about a dozen wedding dresses, each with a price and a description—*A-line, bateau, ivory, organza, Empire.* All words Abby hoped would never invade her personal life.

"You have the cable hookup in here," Carol said. "It was like torture looking at dresses on the dial-up. It took ten minutes just to download one designer."

"The injustice," Delila muttered.

"Oh! You guys can help us decide!" Carol said, standing suddenly and slapping her hands together. "What do you think?"

She picked up a cardboard box from the floor and held it out in front of her. Abby and Delila peeked inside. One half of the box was filled with different silver, gold and chrome bells, each with a ribbon tied at the top. The other half was jammed with little plastic bottles.

"What's that stuff for?" Delila asked.

"At the end of the ceremony as we walk back down the aisle, I'm either gonna have the guests ring these little bells or"—she opened a little white bottle with two hearts on the top and pulled out a bubble wand—"have everyone blow bubbles!" She demonstrated by showering Abby and Delila with said bubbles.

"I thought rice pelting was traditional," Delila said.

"So did I," Tucker said. "Until Carol educated me on the fact that the rice is bad for the birds."

Tucker and Carol exchanged a sickeningly sweet smile and Delila shot Abby an incredulous and pitying look.

"So, what do you guys think, bells or bubbles?" Carol asked. She held one of the bells up next to her face and tinkled it.

"Why don't you just do both?" Delila asked.

Carol clucked her tongue. "Delila, this is serious."

"Right, as opposed to, say, the homeless problem or oppression of women in the Middle East or the perpetual state of war in the Congo," Abby said.

"Or mad cow disease!" Delila added with satisfaction.

Carol's face darkened. "Fine. If you guys don't want to help, I'll just deal with it myself."

Carol placed the box on the floor and sat down at the desk again. Abby let out a sigh of relief. She knew Carol was disappointed, but the idea of helping pick out wedding stuff when Abby wasn't even sure there would *be* a wedding was just a little too depressing. Besides, it was just bubbles and bells. Carol would get over it.

"Don't worry, Carol. We'll figure it out," Tucker said patiently.

"So . . . Ab? The park?" Delila said.

Abby was about to grab her sunscreen and flee when she saw Carol's face crumple.

"Oh! You're going out?" She put her chin down on the back of the desk chair and looked up at them with her big doe eyes. This did not bode well. "I was hoping you'd come with me. Mom and Becky and I have an appointment at Here Comes the Bride."

Abby blanched. "Wedding dresses? Already?"

"Well, we are trying to put a wedding together in just a few weeks," Carol said. "Most people have a year or more. Mom's going to use all her connections to get me a dress right away, but then there are measurements and fittings. . . . I have to order a gown ASAP."

"Okay, I get that. I do," Abby said, backing toward the door as if she were backing away from a rabid animal. "But I have plans. Delila and I were going to go to the park. I mean, if you'd given me some notice . . ."

"Oh! Delila can come, too!" Carol said, grabbing a stack of pictures out of Abby's printer. She stood up and slung her bag over her shoulder. "I'd love another opinion!"

"I'd go, but Carol wants the dress to be a surprise," Tucker said, slipping both arms around Carol and kissing her cheek.

Ick. Does he kiss Melissa *with that mouth?*

"So, Delila?" Carol asked, beaming.

"Uh—that's okay," Delila said, shoving the boom box into Abby's hands. "I just remembered I have to be somewhere that's—not—here."

She turned and rushed down the hall.

"D, don't leave me," Abby said desperately, following after her.

"Sorry, Ab. But wedding dress shopping? I'd

rather eat mud," Delila whispered, halfway down the stairs already. "Call me tonight. If you survive."

A minute later Abby heard the door slam and re-signed herself to her fate. She was a bridesmaid now. Her life was no longer her own.

"Ready?" Carol asked, wrapping her arm around Abby's back. "This is gonna be so much fun!"

Abby looked down at the stereo she was hugging and wondered where it had all gone wrong. Coming home seemed to be the problem these days. She should really consider not doing that anymore.

"Sure," Abby said. She forced a smile so big it actually made her face hurt. "Can't wait."

• • •

"Oh, Abby! You look just beautiful!" her mother trilled, clasping her hands together.

Abby's face was red and blotchy and she was sweating profusely. She could not believe this was happening. For the first two hours everything had been fine. But then Morgan Rice, the owner of the shop, said she had to leave in half an hour. And Carol had freaked out because she wasn't going to get to try on all the ones she liked. "Sometimes girls get their bridesmaids to try on dresses too. That way you still get to see what they look like on, but you save time," Morgan had suggested helpfully. So now here Abby was. Putting on actual wedding dresses.

It was too horrible to be real.

This was only the third dress she had tried on, but the process was giving her more of a workout than any soccer game she'd ever been in. Not only did these things weigh more than she did, but they were impossible to struggle into. Plus it was like every wedding gown on the planet was made with some kind of insulating material that kept her body temperature at an even 110 degrees.

"I look like a cupcake," Abby said. She wiped her brow and stepped in front of the three-way mirror.

Somehow Abby had ended up with all the dresses her mother had picked out. The hoops and the five layers of skirts and the itchy, itchy lace. This was the biggest one yet with a skirt that extended about three feet out in every direction. It weighed a good four hundred pounds and had a train that went on for days. At least her athletic frame could handle it. Abby was sure Carol would buckle under the weight.

"Carol! Come look at this!" her mother called as she and Morgan pinned the dress tightly around her waist. Lace crackled and a pin jabbed Abby in the side.

"Ow!"

Becky stepped out of her dressing room in a tasteful spaghetti-strap dress with a simple skirt and not a poof in sight.

"Oh, Abby! Look at you!" she said. Her hand was over her heart like it was just *overflowing*.

Abby fanned her face with her hands and blew up at her hairline, trying to move the piece of hair that was plastered to her forehead.

"Carol!"

"I'll be right there!" Carol replied.

"Please come out before I melt," Abby pleaded.

Finally the door opened. Carol stuck her head out, took one look at Abby and cracked up laughing. "And the Cheesiest Bride Award goes to . . ."

"Thank you! Get me out of this thing!" Abby said, flapping her arms.

"Carol, this dress is beautiful," her mother said. "Don't you think you should at least try it on yourself before you dismiss it out of hand?"

"Mom, that dress is awful," Carol said. "She looks like a parade float. No offense, Morgan."

"None taken. Everyone has different tastes," Morgan said diplomatically.

"That is exactly the dress I would have worn if I had had a real wedding," Abby's mother said wistfully.

"Yeah, Mom. But that's you. And I'm not you," Carol said.

Abby's mother stiffened, obviously hurt. At the moment, however, Abby couldn't think of anything other than the pin that was digging itself deeper and deeper into her side, and the fact that the heat was starting to make her dizzy.

"Morgan, do you think you could—"

"What about this, Mom?" Carol asked, stepping into full view for the first time.

Becky took one look at her and gasped loudly. "Oh! That is *gorg*eous!" she said. Of course, her opinion didn't hold much cred. She'd said the same thing about every single dress in the store.

Abby pulled the lace collar away from her own neck and fanned at her skin as she studied her sister.

Carol's hair was gathered up in a messy bun and her cheeks were all flushed, but it was her grin that told the tale. Abby knew Carol well enough to realize that her sister thought she'd found *the* dress.

Miraculously, it seemed that the girl had managed to find the one wearable gown in the place. The top was plain with a kind of scoop neck and the skirt was straight. A lace triangle covered only half the skirt at an asymmetrical angle. Definitely modern and semi-cool—for a bridal gown. She could see why her sister liked it.

"Isn't that the same one you just had on?" her mother asked.

Carol slumped slightly, clearly perturbed. "No! The one I just had on was *all* lace."

"Well, I like it," Abby said.

"Yeah?" Carol turned to see the back in the mirror.

"Yeah. Now can someone . . . help me . . . out of this thing?" Abby asked as she grasped in vain for the back clasp. No one even looked at her. The train started to gather up in a twist around her feet as she turned and turned.

"Mom?" Carol said, holding her arms out. "I really think this is it."

Her mother tilted her head to one side. Abby was sweating so much from the exertion that she was starting to smell.

"Really, anyone. Just a little help here," she said, stretching her arms behind her. She felt the clasp beneath her fingers, but it slipped right through them thanks to all the perspiration.

"I just don't understand why you want to wear

something with no shape," her mother said. She walked behind Carol and turned her to face the mirror, then stood behind her. "Don't you want to look like a bride?"

"Mom, we're in a bridal store. All the dresses in here are wedding dresses," Carol said. "I look like a bride."

"That design is all the rage, Phoebe," Morgan said, coming to Carol's rescue. "There are a lot more modern dresses out there these days."

"Becky, maybe?" Abby said desperately as she continued to spin, trying to find the back clasp in the mirror. "All I need is—"

"I know, I know," Abby's mom said. "Believe me, I've seen them. But Carol, just look at Abby! Now *she* looks like a bri—"

Everyone turned to look at Abby as directed and at that moment the train tightened around her feet, binding them together mummy style. As Abby made one last grab for the clasp, her knees knocked into each other, her ankles strained, and before she knew it, she was going down.

"Help!" she called out, arms flailing.

"Omigod!"

Slam! Abby turned her face just in time before her nose broke her fall.

"Ooooow." Abby lifted her chin and moved her bruised jaw around. She looked up, paralyzed by taffeta from the waist down as Becky, Carol, her mother and Morgan all gazed at her in a circle. "Um . . . do you think someone could help me now?"

· 7 ·

The Icing on the Cake

Abby walked into her room that night, exhausted. "They should have an exercise class called cardio-dress-trying-on," she mumbled to herself. "It'd be bigger than Pilates."

At least Carol had made a decision about her dress, placing an order for her first choice. Once everyone had been assured that Abby was okay after her big fall, they had all had a good laugh and Abby's mom had realized she didn't want to be a contender for the Most Horrendous MOB list. She had agreed that Carol's choice was perfect for her and they had all gone to the Watertown Diner for celebratory milk shakes.

Abby smiled as she sat down at her computer. It had turned out to be a fun night in the end. Even if her cheek still hurt. Now she just had to IM Delila and let her know that she had, in fact, lived to tell the tale.

Abby turned on the computer. As the desktop whirred to life, the speakers suddenly blared the classic wedding march, loud enough to wake Wagner himself. Scared out of her skin, Abby grabbed the right speaker and turned down the volume.

"She's got to be kidding me," Abby said. Carol had replaced the pleasant, welcoming bing-bonging sound her computer usually made with *that*? Was the girl on drugs?

Abby shifted in her chair and something sharp stabbed her in the butt. She reached back and pulled out a stack of fabric swatches, all shimmering plaids in an array of colors. The card at the top read "Jim Hjelm Bridesmaids" and the staple that held it all together was bent thanks to the interference of Abby's posterior. Abby grimaced as she flipped through the fabrics. Shimmering plaid? She thought she was going to pick out her own dress.

Okay, the girl is still your sister, Abby thought. *If you freak out, you will only live to regret it.* She tossed the swatches on her bed and turned back to her computer. Her mouth dropped open in horror.

Her desktop—previously a black screen with a picture of the U.S. Women's World Cup soccer team in the center—was now a light blue background with little white hearts all over it. Wedding bells blinked all around the edges of the screen and there, right smack in the middle, were two cartoon kids with huge wide eyes, dressed up in wedding garb, smiling out at her. Clenching her jaw, Abby grabbed the mouse and clicked on the preferences tab to change the whole thing back, but nowhere in her files could she find the World Cup photo. It was gone. Erased. Replaced by cherubic wedding gnomes.

"Carol!" she shouted. She whirled around just as the culprit herself walked right into the room with a cardboard box in her hands. No knock. No nothing.

"Hey! I was just coming to talk to you about gifts—"

"What did you do to my computer?"

"Oh, I know. Isn't it totally adorable?" Carol said with a grin. She placed the box down on Abby's bed.

Totally adorable? Since when does Carol use the word adorable*?*

"Are you kidding me? Carol, has it escaped your mind that this is *my* computer? *My* room?"

Carol's face changed from repentant to irritated. "I think you're overreacting a little, Ab."

"Look, I said I would help you with the wedding stuff, but this is getting ridiculous."

"Come on—"

"No! Look at my room! And today? Trying on wedding dresses?"

"Okay, okay! I'm sorry," Carol said. "I promise I won't ask you to do anything else above and beyond the call of duty."

Abby eyed her sister, unconvinced. She had a

feeling that brides had a different definition of "call of duty" than most rational people.

"Now, I was wondering if you would mind keeping track of the engagement gifts as they come in," Carol said cautiously. "It just means keeping a list of each present and who it's from so I can write thank-you cards later. Is that cool?"

"Yeah. I guess I can do that," Abby said.

"Great," Carol said. "That would be a huge help."

Abby smiled. List keeping was simple and straightforward and sounded much more like a traditional maid of honor duty than the bridal gown torture of that afternoon. Maybe Carol hadn't completely gone over the edge.

"Good. So . . . what's in there?" she asked, looking warily at the box on her bed.

"Oh! I narrowed it down to one of these ten bottles of bubbles," Carol said, picking up the box and holding it out to Abby. "Could you test all of them and let me know which ones bubble the best? That'd be great."

Abby looked down at the box of little plastic bottles. "Which ones—"

"Make the best bubbles, you know," Carol said, lifting one shoulder. "It all varies based on the bubble formula and the size of the wand. I mean, what's the point of ordering bubbles if they're just going to pop the second you blow on them, right? I need to order them tomorrow, so let me know. Thanks, Ab!"

Carol twirled out of the room with a grin, closing the door behind her. Abby stared after her for a moment, totally baffled. Just when she thought her sister was on the rational train, she took a detour right into Cuckooville.

Abby stalked over to her closet and chucked the whole box in on top of her sneakers and shoes, then slammed the door and slapped her hands together with satisfaction.

Abby: 1
Bubbles: 0

•   •   •

"The invitation is a first impression for your wedding," Abby's father said sagely. "It tells your guests what kind of party to expect the moment they open the envelope. It's one of the most important elements."

Carol, Abby and Tucker sat on a hard bench on one side of a huge table, looking up at him with big, blank stares. The stationery store's main table was covered with hulking binders, each one packed with invitation examples ranging from the elegant to the kitschy to the just plain corny.

"You have an important decision to make here today, you two," he said, his brow furrows deepening as he looked from Carol to Tucker. "Make no mistake about it."

"He couldn't be barbecue-obsessed like other dads," Abby said under her breath when her father turned away to request a specific sample book. "No. Our dad has to have adamant views on card stock and vellum finishes."

Carol snorted a laugh and she and Abby shared a smile.

"Yeah, our dads are definitely different breeds," Tucker put in. "Clint Robb would probably break out in hives if he even walked into this place."

Carol slipped her arm through Tucker's and gave him a squeeze. Abby swallowed hard. Whenever Abby was around Tucker her stomach started hurting and she started obsessing about the conversation she had overheard. What was she supposed to do? Abby's uncertainty only irritated her and that irritation, coupled with her ire toward Tucker, conspired to make her entirely miserable, angry, guilty and anxious whenever he was in the room. But she couldn't *look* upset or Carol would get upset. And Abby didn't want to make Carol any crazier than she already was until she was sure there was something Carol needed to be crazy about. It was all so complicated it made Abby's upcoming U.S. Government final look like a cakewalk.

"Take a look at these," Abby's father said, placing a large red book in front of them. "This is my favorite designer. Her stuff is really original."

Carol opened the book as their dad hovered over her with an expectant smile. The first invitation was square with a pink-and-white-striped border and a white card in the center that held all the wedding information. The flap of the envelope was striped as well and the RSVP card was circular and looked like a peppermint candy.

"These are wedding invitations?" Tucker asked. "They're so cool."

Carol flipped the page. The next invite was a sun-flower theme, just as over-the-top with the invite cut out along the edges in the shape of petals. As Carol continued to flip, Abby's heart continued to sink. There were starfish, sailboats, flip-flops, hearts, top hats, and champagne glasses. The invitations were adorable—if you liked that kind of thing.

Tucker did. "Oh, *sweet*! A cowboy boot!" he said excitedly.

"I knew you'd like them," Abby's father said, beaming.

"Can we get the cowboy boot? How cool is that?" Tucker asked, looking at Carol with a childlike hope in his eyes. Suddenly Abby was able to picture exactly how Tucker looked at age five. Abby couldn't believe he was suggesting to Carol that they use cowboy boot invitations for their wedding. Didn't he know her sister at all?

Maybe Melissa *would be down with cutesy invites,* Abby thought. *But not Carol.*

"Tucker, I let you have those Save the Date cards . . . ," Carol began.

"I thought you liked those," Tucker said.

"I did. They were cute. But this is the actual invitation," Carol said patiently. "We're not having a kid's birthday party. We're having a wedding."

"You want something more sophisticated. I get it," Tucker said, nodding. "Okay."

"Wait a minute," Abby's dad said. "A wedding invitation doesn't have to be—"

"Actually, Dad, I kind of already found one I like," Carol interrupted, handing the big red book over to Abby. Carol pulled another book over to her—a standard gray one—and flipped to a page toward the back. "See?" she said, tilting the book up.

Her father put on his glasses and bent over the page. The invitation was ivory-colored and square with a single satin ribbon tied in a small and tasteful bow at the top. The wording was printed in a simple, classic font in the center and all the other pieces were just as plain and elegant.

Abby was not surprised. Carol had picked an invitation that was very her.

"I like it," Tucker said.

"It's kind of boring, isn't it?" her father asked, standing up straight.

"No," Carol said, looking down at the book. "I think it's pretty."

The front door opened and Abby's mother walked in, all flustered. "I'm so sorry I'm late. I just spent two hours at the synagogue trying to get Rabbi Schaer to co-officiate the Wentworth–Schwartz wedding and that man can really talk." She paused for breath. "Did you pick something already?" She sounded disappointed.

Carol turned the book toward her mother with a hopeful smile and Abby crossed her fingers. But her mom glanced down at Carol's selection and made a dubious face. "Square, Carol? Really?"

Carol sighed. "What's wrong with square?"

"I was thinking something more traditional," her mother said. "You know, a four-by-six card." She reached out, grabbed a book and opened it right to a page with seriously boring, white, oblong cards.

"Oh, Phoebe, come on," Abby's father scoffed.

Here we go, Abby thought.

Her mother rolled her eyes. "I suppose you want her to get something shaped like a martini glass or a high heel."

"If that's what she wants," her father said.

Carol attempted to interject. "Actually I—"

"Oh for goodness' sake. That's not what Carol wants!" her mother said, her voice rising. "Do you want our daughter's wedding to look like a carnival?"

"Do you want our daughter's wedding to look like a funeral?" her father shot back. "Actually, it may as well be a funeral with your boring relatives showing up."

Abby's mother slapped the book of invites closed. "Well, at least we don't have to worry about *my* family using the chandeliers as swings!"

Abby's father turned purple. "That happened *one* time," he said, lifting a finger. "And you were the one who ordered the good scotch."

"Like it really mattered to those lushes?"

"Um . . . you guys?" Abby said, glancing around at the dozen or so people who were staring at them, slack-jawed.

"Not now, Abby," they said in unison.

Abby's heart thumped and she glanced at Carol, who stood up and tried to intervene.

"This does not look good," Tucker said as Carol ushered her parents to the front of the store.

Ugh! He's going to try to bond with me again, isn't he? Abby thought.

"Maybe you should go help her," Abby suggested.

"Good point," Tucker said.

"Yes! Go! Your bride needs you," Abby replied, shooing him away.

Left alone at the table while her family argued, Abby felt more than a little conspicuous. She got up slowly and moved off, pretending to be interested in the guest books that were lined up on glass shelves near the wall.

"They're a little stressed out about the wedding," Abby said to a mother-and-daughter pair near the back of the store who were gaping at her family. The mother sniffed, like she was so superior, and returned to filling out an order form. The daughter, however, leaned toward Abby and spoke through her teeth.

"For my parents, it was the uneven number of ushers to bridesmaids," she said quietly. "That's what made *them* snap."

Abby nodded. Then she found her way to a chair in the corner and sat down to wait out the power struggle. She had a feeling this could take a while. A little kid next to her swung his legs while working diligently away at a Game Boy. Smart kid. At least he'd come prepared.

"Can I borrow that when you're done?" Abby asked.

Carol Marie Beaumont

Possible Invitation Wordings

Mr. and Mrs. David Beaumont
Request the honor of your presence
At the marriage of their daughter
Carol Marie
To
Tucker Clint Robb
Saturday, August first

If Tucker wants his parents mentioned . . .

Mr. and Mrs. David Beaumont
Request the honor of your presence
At the marriage of their daughter
Carol Marie
To
Tucker Clint Robb
Son of
Mr. Clint Robb and Ms. Mary McKee
Saturday, August first

But if his stepmom needs to be mentioned . . . .

Mr. and Mrs. David Beaumont
Request the honor of your presence
At the marriage of their daughter
Carol Marie

To
Tucker Clint Robb
Son of
Mr. and Mrs. Clint Robb
and
Ms. Mary McKee
Saturday, August first

But he's not technically his stepmom's son and his mother would probably freak if the stepmom was mentioned before her, so . . .

Mr. and Mrs. David Beaumont
Request the honor of your presence
At the marriage of their daughter
Carol Marie
To
Tucker Clint Robb
Son of
Mr. Clint Robb and Ms. Mary McKee
And stepson of
Ms. Sharon Robb
Saturday, August first

??? Okay, that's just TOO MUCH INFORMATION!!!

How about this?

Carol and Tucker are getting married.
Come see.
Saturday, August 1st

• • •

Abby pulled into the driveway and was psyched to see Tessa Leone's black VW Bug parked next to her mom's Avalon. It was the next day and Abby was supposed to be meeting with Tessa and Missy Marx, Carol's two best friends from Harvard, to talk about the bridal shower. Normally such a task would send Abby into dry-heave territory, but Tessa was totally cool. She was a student athlete on the Harvard volleyball team and, unlike some of Carol's other friends, she never talked down to Abby, never made her feel inferior. If there was anyone who was going to be with Abby on the whole Carol-is-jumping-the-gun thing, it was Tessa. Maybe she had even shown up early to talk Carol out of it! Then Abby wouldn't have to tell Carol about Tucker's possible indiscretions. And Abby's parents would stop being crazy. And her room would start looking like her room again. And Tucker would go on back to Colorado. And everything would be just fine!

One could dream.

Abby slammed the door of the van and raced right upstairs. She could hear voices coming from Carol's room so she barreled right in. What she saw in front of her nearly made her keep going—straight through the room and out the window.

Carol sat on her bed grinning up at Tessa and Missy, who were standing in the center of the room wearing the most awful dresses Abby had ever seen. They were blue-and-white shimmering plaid and strapless, with blue ribbons around the waists. The girls looked as if they had just stepped off the set of

Grease. A weird version where everyone's clothes were supershiny.

"Abby!" Tessa cried, grabbing her into a hug. Abby just stood there, arms down at her sides. Then Tessa pulled back and struck a pose, pulling her long dark hair over her shoulder. "Well? What do you think?"

Missy executed a twirl. "I love the way they spin!"

"What are they?" Abby asked. Maybe Missy and Tessa *were* doing *Grease.*

"They're our bridesmaids' dresses," Tessa said. "Missy found out that this place in Boston was having a secret sale so we went over there this morning and they actually had one in each of our sizes." She went to the closet and pulled out yet another offensive frock, holding it out to Abby. "You're an eight, right?"

Abby's heart dropped. This was wrong on so many levels. Not only had Carol promised her that she would get to pick out her own dress, but wasn't Abby the sister here? The true best friend? The maid of honor? The other bridesmaids weren't supposed to go around picking out dresses without her, were they?

"Carol, what's going on?" Abby asked.

"Don't freak out," Carol said, standing. "They didn't even tell me they were doing this."

Missy's brow creased. "Yeah, but this is the dress you wanted, right, Carol?" she asked. "The iridescent plaid in sky. That's what you told us on the phone last week."

"Oh, God. Did we get the wrong thing?" Tessa asked.

Abby felt like a furnace was about to explode inside her head. Carol was in on this travesty? "You decided on bridesmaids' dresses without me? You went behind my back and told *them* what we were all going to be wearing?" she demanded. "Carol, how could you do this?"

"Abby, listen–"

"No! All I've done for the past few weeks is plan your wedding!" Abby said. "You swore I wasn't going to have to do anything, but instead every single second of my free time has been taken up with songs and gifts and favors and bubbles and invitations and gowns. And the *one* thing I *really* cared about was that I got to pick my own dress. You promised me I could. God, Carol, can't you think about anyone other than yourself for five seconds?"

Carol looked as if she had been slapped. There was a moment of silence that only made Abby fume. Was it so insane of her to expect her sister to make good on *one* promise? Carol was leaving her in less than three weeks to go off and live on the other side of the country with a perfect stranger. *And forever after everything would be completely and totally different.* Couldn't she at least give Abby this one thing?

"Abby, look, I think you're forgetting that this is your sister's wedding," Tessa said calmly, stepping forward. "It's not unreasonable of her to ask you to wear what she wants."

Abby was mortified to the core. It was the first time Tessa had ever said anything remotely condescending in the four years she'd known her. This wedding was turning everyone into someone else.

"You wear it," Abby said, backing toward the door. "That dress is not coming anywhere near me."

"Abby!" Carol said.

"You promised me," Abby said, glaring at her. "But clearly that doesn't mean anything to you anymore."

"Abby! We're supposed to talk about the shower!" Missy called after her.

But Abby just started running, down the stairs and out the door. Obviously Carol didn't value her opinion or her feelings. If Tessa and Missy were so important that they got to be in on wardrobe decisions while Abby was left out, then they could plan the shower without her as well. Let them deal with the Bridezilla for a while.

• • •

"I can't believe you did that," Carol said as she drove the van through the downtown shopping area on Saturday afternoon. She kept looking at Abby accusingly, then back at the road, clearly fighting between wanting to yell at Abby and wanting to keep them from slamming into any pedestrians. "I mentioned to Tessa and Missy last week that I really liked those dresses, but I never told them to go out and *buy* them."

"But you want me to wear it, right?" Abby replied. "You want me, a person who cringes every time I put on my stupid school uniform pleats, to wear that big-skirted, strapless, shiny . . . thing."

"So what if I do? Is that so wrong? It's one day, Abby! *My* day!"

"I get it, all right! It's all about Carol!" Abby

shouted back. "But you promised me I could wear what I wanted to wear."

"Oh my God! You with the promises!" Carol replied. "Do you have any idea how childish you sound?"

Abby's mouth dropped open. "I'm childish? For what? For expecting you not to lie to me? Besides, you're the one walking around acting like a queen just because some guy asked you to marry him."

"Tucker is not just some guy," Carol said, suddenly sounding eerily calm. "He's the most wonderful man in the world."

Abby's stomach dropped to her feet. *I have to tell her,* Abby thought. And she suddenly felt as if she was about to vomit. They drove along in tense silence. Abby kept willing herself to speak, to open her mouth and tell Carol that the most wonderful man in the world might just be the biggest jerk ever.

"Carol," Abby started. "Actually, I–"

Without warning Carol slammed on the brakes. And she turned to Abby with a look on her face unlike anything Abby had ever seen before. Her eyes were cold and hard. She opened her mouth and spoke with a voice that was a cross between a whisper and a scream. "Abigail. I have listened to you act like a spoiled brat ever since I first told you my happy news. I'm sorry if my wedding is a nuisance for you, but if you say one more word, I mean even *one more word,* to try and ruin this for me, I will never *ever* forgive you." Carol was clenching the steering wheel so tightly her knuckles were white.

Abby felt her fingers tingling and her head pounding. "Carol—"

"And *that* is a promise I intend to keep." Abby had no idea what to say. She wanted to continue, but she didn't know how she could. So she sat there in miserable silence. After a few minutes Carol turned to her again, her voice softened.

"Look, I'm sorry. But Tucker's meeting us here after he's done at the tux place and I really don't want him to see you acting like this," Carol said.

"Oh really? So then what *exactly* do you want him to see me acting like?" Abby replied. She suddenly felt like she was about to cry. She clenched her teeth and blinked hard.

"This is insane, Abby," Carol said. She hit the gas and zoomed into the parking lot in front of Spencer's Bakery. "For once, baby sister, all the attention is on me, and you can't take it."

Abby blinked. "Wait a minute, what? Are you saying I'm *jealous*?"

"Hey! You said it, not me!" Carol said.

"That doesn't even make any sense!" Abby replied.

"Oh *please*!" Carol shrieked. "It's so obvious what this is all about. You're the baby! You've always been the focus of our family. Now it's my turn and you don't know what to do with yourself."

"You are soooooo out of line right now," Abby said. "And I swear if you call me baby one more time—"

"All I'm saying is this day is going to be mine.

Mine, mine, mine," Carol said. "And you'd better accept that soon or we're all gonna be pretty miserable."

Carol got out of the van and slammed the door extra hard. Abby had to sit there for a moment to catch her breath and calm herself. Carol had clearly lost her mind. Had she really just threatened to never speak to Abby again, gotten half-over it a second later and then a second after that uttered the words "mine, mine, mine"? It was official. The girl was a Bridezilla.

"If I hear the word *I* come out of her mouth one more time today, I will not be responsible for my actions," Abby muttered, climbing out of the van. She straightened her denim jacket, swung her hair behind her shoulders and walked into the bakery.

"Abigail! How are you?" Noah's father, Dominic, greeted her from behind the counter. He was a tall man with salt-and-pepper hair and huge forearms, his face deeply tan and very wrinkled. But even though he looked imposing, his eyes were always bright and he was always ready with a smile, like today. He was loading muffins into a box for a customer as she walked in. "Noah and Carol went to the back with your sister's fella. Go ahead," he told her.

"Thanks, Mr. Spencer," Abby said as she slipped behind the counter.

The bakery kitchen was bustling, getting ready for a busy Sunday morning. Through the haze of flour, Abby saw Carol, Tucker and Noah sitting at the table in the back corner. There was a tray of miniature cakes and full-size slices between them. Abby walked over and plopped into the free chair, slumping down until her butt hung off the edge.

She was so confused and upset she didn't even remember to obsess about the he-loves-me, he-loves-me-not situation. Right now, all wedding-related people were the enemy—Noah included.

"Abby! You're looking especially grumpy today," Noah said brightly.

"Trust me. You don't want to start with her," Carol said.

I'm going to kill her, Abby thought. Tucker shot her a concerned "What's wrong?" look. Abby looked away as if she hadn't noticed.

"Can we just get started, Noah?" Carol asked, ignoring her.

"All right then!" Noah said. "We have a bunch of different examples here, not that you guys haven't tasted all our cakes in the past, but any excuse for a tasting, right?"

"They all look awesome," Tucker said. "What's that one?"

"That's a basic vanilla cake with lemon frosting," Noah said. "The lemon is very subtle, but it just adds a little something."

Abby picked up a fork and took a big hunk out of the cake.

"Abby!" Carol said.

But the bite was already gone. Abby swallowed and pulled the fork slowly out of her mouth, making sure she got all the icing.

"Yum!" Abby said with a smile. Over the years

the two of them had turned sisterly battling into an art form.

"Pardon my sister. Apparently she's PMSing," Carol said.

"Carol!" Abby looked at Noah, mortified. "I am not—"

"Noah, we were thinking about doing carrot cake," Carol said, cutting Abby off. "You guys make the best. I've loved it since I was a kid."

"We could do that," Noah said, making a note on his clipboard. "I have a slice here if you want to—"

"Carrot cake?" Abby blurted out. "Carol, no one *likes* carrot cake. It's *vegetable* cake. You can't serve vegetables for dessert!"

"Plenty of people like carrot cake, Abby," Tucker said.

"Like who?"

"Like me!" Carol said. "I like carrot cake."

There it was. The *I* Abby was waiting for. "Yeah? Well, that's because you're a *freak*!"

"What is wrong with you?" Carol asked, turning in her chair. "This is *my* wedding cake."

"Me, me, me, my, my, my," Abby said, shaking her head back and forth. "What is it with brides that they suddenly forget about all the other pronouns? Do they knock them out of your head at the first dress fitting or something?"

Carol's mouth hung open as she stared at Abby. "Are you saying I'm *selfish*?"

"If the crinoline fits," Abby said, folding her arms over her chest.

"Um . . . guys?" Tucker said, glancing at Noah. "Let's calm down a little, here."

"Abby, come on," Noah said. "It's *her* wedding. Besides, I like carrot cake, too. I'd eat it."

Abby whirled on him. She was so sick of him taking everyone else's side. Couldn't he let her be right even just once?

"Oh yeah?" she said, her temper getting the better of her. She picked up the piece of carrot cake, the cream cheese icing smushing between her fingers. "You like it so much? Here!"

Before she even knew what she was doing, she had mashed the entire hunk of cake and icing into his face. Carol gasped. Tucker backed up his chair. Crumbs tumbled down Noah's shirt and blobs of icing dropped onto the table. Noah licked the cake around his mouth, then pressed his lips together. Abby held her breath. What had she just done?

"You, my friend, are *so* dead," Noah said.

Abby stood up, knocking her chair over, and then the cake started to fly. Noah picked up a slice of chocolate-on-chocolate and threw it right at her chest, where it exploded. Abby snatched for a piece with meringue filling and it came apart in her hands, giving her double the ammo. As the two of them assaulted each other, Tucker grabbed Carol's hand and pulled her out of the way, giving Noah room to come around the table. Abby tried to dodge, but Noah was too fast. He grabbed the back of her head and mashed a slice of cannoli cream cake in her face, rubbing it into her cheeks and along her forehead.

Abby laughed and screeched and protested. She reached over blindly and picked up a piece of red velvet cake, then slapped it into the back of Noah's head with a splat. She worked the icing into his hair with her fingers and Noah groaned in disgust. Abby giggled uncontrollably. All of her frustration about the wedding and her parents and Italy faded away as the two of them cracked up laughing, clinging to each other for fear of letting go and being assaulted again.

"You two have totally lost it," Carol said.

Then Noah broke off and ran across the kitchen and Abby gave chase, screeching and wielding the last piece of cake.

It was more fun than she'd had in days.

"Stop! Stop stop stop!" Carol shouted at the top of her lungs.

Still laughing, Abby turned around to look at her sister and Tucker. Most of the bakery workers had long since moved out of the line of fire to avoid getting splattered. Carol and Tucker were the only people on their side of the room and Carol's face was so red and blotchy she might have just run a mile. Her hands were curled into fists down at her sides, like a kid about to throw a tantrum.

"Maybe you just need a piece of cake," Abby said. And before she knew what was happening, the last piece of cake flew through the air and smacked Carol in the chest.

Noah and Tucker looked shocked. Abby let out a nervous giggle. This was exactly the type of shenanigan her sister normally enjoyed. Food fights, paint fights, splashing fights, pillow fights. When it came to mayhem of this variety, Carol was almost always the instigator. Only now she didn't look that amused.

"You . . . ," Carol said slowly, on the verge of total eruption. "You are the worst maid of honor *ever!*"

Abby's mouth dropped open slightly. "Carol—"

"Forget it," Carol said. "Come on, Tucker. Let's go."

Then she turned around and stormed out of the kitchen, and Tucker, after shooting Abby an apologetic look, followed. Abby was left with her mouth hanging open, covered in ten kinds of icing.

Slowly, Noah stood up from behind the counter he'd been using for protection. He looked at Abby sympathetically, apologetically—his deep blue eyes uncharacteristically serious. And even though Abby's insides were tied in guilty knots, something happened within her chest. She looked at Noah and her heart responded. It thumped like it wanted out. Or like it wanted to pull her over to him by force.

Icing was a good look for Noah. A *really* good look.

Noah lifted the corner of his apron and wiped a streak of pink icing from her cheek. Excited tingles ran all down her face, into her neck and straight down to her toes.

"You okay?" he asked.

"I'm fine," she said, taking an instinctive step back like she always did when she felt that zip of attraction for him.

Was she just imagining it, or was he looking at her

differently? Looking at her like maybe he felt it too? Maybe it was just the glob of white icing across his forehead, but his eyes were *so* blue. And they were staring right at her.

"I'm out of cake," Noah said, misinterpreting her step back as a battle defense.

Abby laughed and it came out as a snort, which made Noah laugh as well.

"So. Carol was pretty angry," Noah said.

"Yeah," Abby said as icing dried to her face. "Apparently I'm the worst maid of honor . . . *ever.*"

She looked at Noah and suddenly she couldn't take it anymore. She burst out laughing and took him right with her. Before long they were both clutching their stomachs, gasping for breath, with tears streaming down their faces.

"I'm the worst maid of honor ever!" Abby cheered, throwing her arms in the air. Noah and the bakery workers shouted and clapped. Abby swiped a blob of chocolate off her chest and held it up. "Here's to me!" she said, and sucked it off her finger.

Noah grinned at her, and Abby could have sworn there was real admiration in his eyes. Things were about to get a lot more interesting.

· 8 ·

Forsaking All Others

"I thought you two were gonna strangle each other," Noah said, half an hour into their postwar cleanup. He crossed to the sink to rinse out an icing-covered rag and Abby followed.

"Yeah . . . we haven't fought like this since we were kids," she said. She leaned back into the table and pushed a curl behind her ear. "I don't know what's going on."

"Separation anxiety, probably," Noah said. He wrung out the rag and hung it over the faucet. "I mean, once she's married, she's probably gonna move, right?"

Abby's heart squeezed unexpectedly and painfully. She knew Carol was leaving, but she hadn't really allowed herself to think much about what would actually *happen* after the wedding. The pure insanity of the event itself, of her parents' reaction to it and Carol's Bridezilla status, were upsetting enough. What would life be like when Carol was gone? When she wasn't just an hour away by car? When actual plane tickets would have to be purchased and Abby would have to go through eighteen security checkpoints at the airport just to get to her?

"So, what? We're fighting because we're never going to see each other again?" Abby asked.

"You're not never going to see each other again," Noah said in a soothing voice. "You're just fighting because the idea of being far apart is stressing you out. It's like a defense mechanism. If you fight you can pretend to yourselves that you don't like each other and then you won't miss each other so much."

"What are you, a psychologist all of a sudden?"

"Yeah. That'll be a hundred bucks," Noah said. Abby laughed. "All I'm saying is, maybe you should keep that in mind before you freak out again. Things are crazy right now, but when it's all over Carol's going to be happily married and you're going to have a new brother-in-law."

Abby looked at the floor. She still couldn't figure out what to make of Tucker Robb. He seemed like Mr. Perfect most of the time, being genuinely polite to everyone and making Carol ridiculously happy. But what was the odd behavior about? Was Tucker up to something evil or was Abby just imagining it because of this whole upcoming separation thing?

"What?" Noah asked. He leaned back against the table next to her, his arm brushed hers and she flushed.

"It's just . . . Tucker . . ."

"Still don't like the guy, huh?"

"I heard him on the phone," Abby said, biting her lip. "He was talking with some girl named Melissa . . . begging her for another chance or something. I don't know."

The details of the conversation had been fading in Abby's mind and she was starting to get that too-far-from-the-incident doubt. Like maybe she had imagined the whole thing.

"You listened in on his phone call?"

"No! You make it sound like I picked up the line!" Abby said. "I just overheard him."

"Ah," Noah said, nodding.

"So? What should I do? Should I tell Carol?" Abby asked. "I mean, I sort of tried to start telling her but she totally flipped as soon as I mentioned Tucker's name so—"

"No. Don't tell Carol," Noah said. He stood up straight and faced her so she could look at his perfect blue eyes again. "At least not until you know more."

Abby blinked and stood up herself. "So . . . what? I should spy on him?"

"No, freakshow, you should not spy on him," Noah said. "If you're really concerned about it, talk to the guy. You're probably jumping to conclusions, and if he really loves your sister he'll appreciate the fact that you cared enough to ask."

Noah's speech brought Abby back to earth in more ways than one. First of all, as often seemed to be the case, Noah was right. Tucker *was* the person to go to. Now that he'd mentioned it, it seemed like such an obvious thing to do. If there was a logical explanation, she would avoid getting her sister all worked up over nothing. If there wasn't a logical explanation, Abby could make Tucker fess up himself, which he should do anyway.

Secondly, Noah had just called her freakshow. Not that this was out of the ordinary. It was perfectly within the realms of normal. But it made it painfully clear what she'd already known to begin with—Noah's attraction to her did not exist. She'd so wanted to believe Christopher, and she'd so wanted a distraction from this wedding mess that she'd let herself be convinced of something that was so clearly not true. She felt her face flush just thinking about how ridiculous she'd been to even consider that he might. Obviously to him she was still just annoying little Abby Beaumont from the Dove's Roost. And that's all she'd ever be.

• • •

Abby walked into her house, closed the door behind her and sighed. She felt like she'd been run over by a truck, no, by a wedding-mobile. Between the fight with her sister, worrying about Tucker, the wedding planning and the Noah confusion, she felt as if she were losing her mind. And she was beyond exhausted.

She trudged into the kitchen and paused. There, spread out across the kitchen table, were a dozen eight-by-ten black and white photos of Carol and Tucker. Engagement photos, clearly. Abby grimaced at the sight of the two of them, grinning for the camera. In the worst of the set, their foreheads were touching, but their faces were turned at a slight angle toward the camera and they both had these sexy sort of smirks on their faces. Like they were thinking about what they were going to do back in their bedroom after the photo shoot.

"Make me vomit," Abby said. She just couldn't escape no matter what she did. She gathered up all the pictures and placed them facedown in a pile.

The sound of footsteps on the stairs announced Carol's near arrival. All the muscles in Abby's body tensed. The light flicked on and Carol stopped in the doorway at the sight of Abby standing there.

"Hey," Carol said.

"Hey."

"Abby, look, I don't want to get into a whole emotional thing right now. I'm just too tired," Carol said.

"Me too," Abby replied.

"But I have to ask you, what was all that about today?" Carol said. "It can't all be about the dress and I know it's not about cake."

Abby blinked, surprised by tears that suddenly prickled at her eyes. "Can we not do this right now?"

"No. Abby, clearly something's bothering you," Carol said firmly. "What is it? What?"

"Carol," Abby said, her heart full. "I just–"

"Abby, what?"

"You're leaving, all right?" Abby blurted out. "You're leaving and you're going to Colorado and you're leaving me here all by myself and you're— you're happy about it!"

Whoa. Where did that come from? Abby thought.

"Wow," Carol said, pulling out a chair and sitting down. "Is that really how you feel?"

"I–I don't know," Abby said. She took a deep breath and sat down across from Carol, her knees quaking. "I was just so looking forward to you coming home and spending the whole summer with you and then you show up and you tell me you're leaving for some guy I don't even know. It just . . ."

"Sucked," Carol supplied.

Abby smiled wanly. "Yeah. Kind of."

"Wow," Carol said again, looking dazed. "I'm sorry. I guess I never thought of it that way. From your perspective, I mean."

"Yeah, well, why would you? You've got a lot of other things on your mind."

Carol sat forward and looked Abby in the eye. "But you have to know that I'm not happy to be moving away from you," Carol said. "I'm happy to be getting married, but I'm not happy that we're going to be so far apart."

So stay, Abby thought, but knew she couldn't say it. "I know," she said instead.

"And no matter where I live we're always going to be sisters," Carol said. "We're always going to be friends, right?"

Abby had to strain to hold the tears back. She was going to miss Carol so much it hurt already and she was still right in front of her. "Right," Abby said.

"We'll just have to get second jobs to deal with the long-distance bills," Carol joked.

"Ooh! Maybe we can get Mom and Dad to spring for nationwide cell plans!"

"Now you're thinking!" Carol said with a smile. They looked at each other for a moment and Abby felt a strange mix of relief and sorrow. Relief because she had gotten a big chunk of how she was feeling off her chest. Sorrow because Carol was still going to go.

"You know what? You *can* pick out your dress," Carol said finally. "I made a promise and I shouldn't have gone back on it."

"Seriously?" Abby asked, surprised.

"Yeah. Just make it blue, okay?" Carol said. "That way it'll at least match Tessa and Missy's dresses. You're cool with blue, right?"

"There is absolutely nothing wrong with blue," Abby replied with a big smile.

"Good," Carol said, getting up. "Now c'mere. I know you hate the mushy stuff, but you're getting a hug right now."

Abby quite willingly stood and let Carol wrap her up in her arms. She squeezed back tightly and closed her eyes.

"I'm sorry about the cake fight," she said over her sister's shoulder. "And for calling you selfish. I mean, you *are* the bride, right?"

"God, it's still weird to think that," Carol said, pulling back. "I'm a bride."

Abby swallowed back a tight feeling in her throat. Her sister was a bride. And that meant Abby had to stop thinking that everything bride-related was evil. Because Carol was definitely not evil.

"Okay, I'm going to go get the CDs out of my car," Carol said. "You're gonna burn them tomorrow, right?"

Abby smiled. Carol had decided to give out mixed CDs as a wedding favor. She'd put Abby in charge of making them. "Yep," Abby said. "I'm on it."

Carol slipped out and Abby stood there for a moment, looking at the closed door. What would it really be like when there was no possibility of Carol coming through it? Of her surprising them all by joining them for dinner? Of her calling Abby up to go on an impromptu shopping spree in Boston?

Abby felt her chest tighten involuntarily. She stood up straight, rolled her shoulders back and resolved not to wallow. From this moment on she was going to be glad for her sister. She would do everything she could to help her have an amazing wedding. If she was going to send Carol off to Colorado, she was going to send her off happy.

• • •

A few hours later Abby was studying for her English final when she realized she had never eaten dinner. Carol and Tucker had gone out to eat with some friends in Boston and had just returned a few minutes ago. Her parents had been working the Stevenson–Hallgren wedding all night.

Stevenson–Hallgren, Abby thought, sitting up on her bed. *Oooh. They were going to have chicken parmesan, weren't they?*

The very thought of Rocco's sauce made her stomach grumble. Abby laid her book aside and headed downstairs to pilfer some of the leftovers. All the lights were off in the residence, but Abby could still hear the sounds of washing and cleaning coming from the catering kitchen in the Roost. She opened the door at the far end of the living room, which led her to the back hallway of the Dove's Roost Chateau. She was walking by her mother's office when she heard something that made her heart seize up. Was her mother in there . . . *crying?*

Abby leaned back to peek around the open door. And there was her mom, sitting in her chair with her fingertips pressed to her mouth, tears streaking down her face. For a moment Abby was frozen by shock. Her mother was always bursting into happy tears for brides and grooms, but this was different. This was scary.

"Mom?" Abby said uncertainly. "What's wrong?"

Her mother looked up, surprised, and quickly wiped her face with both hands. "I didn't think anybody was home." She picked up her pen and pulled her chair closer to her desk.

"Mom, you're crying," Abby said. She took a couple of steps into the dim room. The only light came from the soft bulb in the lamp on the desk. "What happened?"

"Oh, it's nothing," her mother said, shaking her head. She didn't look up. "It's just . . . your father."

A shot of fear slammed through Abby's chest. "Dad?"

"We had a fight," Abby's mother said, writing rapidly. "It's just . . . sometimes, Abby, I think that man doesn't understand me at all."

"Mom, come on," Abby said with a forced laugh. "You guys are . . . *you*. You're always finishing each other's sentences. He understands you, trust me."

Abby's mother took a deep breath and shook her head again, then continued to write. Abby didn't like this at all.

"What did you fight about?" she asked.

"He wants nouvelle cuisine at the cocktail hour." Abby's mother finally looked at her, wide-eyed. "Can you believe that? He won't budge an inch about it."

"Wait a minute. That's what this is about? You're this upset over Carol's hors d'oeuvres?"

"It's not just that, Abby," her mother said firmly. "That's just an example. It's a symptom."

"A symptom of what?" This was just too much. Her parents couldn't be this crazed over a wedding. Weren't adults supposed to be the rational ones?

Her mother sighed. "You wouldn't understand because you've never been in a relationship," she said, grabbing her pen again. "Wait until you're older and have had more life experience. Then you'll know what I mean."

Abby clenched her jaw. This argument was making her ill. She hated when adults acted so *adult*, like there were certain feelings a person could only have over age thirty, and anyone younger just couldn't comprehend. Abby was trying to help and her mother was dismissing her like she was eight. Meanwhile she was the one getting in a fight over pigs in blankets.

Abby took a deep breath. Part of her wanted to protest, but more of her wanted her mom to stop crying. *Act like an adult here, Abby,* she told herself. *Someone needs to.*

"Anything I can do?"

"I don't think so," her mother said. "But thanks for asking."

"Okay," Abby said, turning around slowly. "See you in the morning?"

"Sure, honey."

Abby walked out, feeling numb. Forget dinner—suddenly she'd lost her appetite. When she got upstairs, she glanced out the back window and saw her father sitting on one of the stone benches, hanging his head.

"I'm never getting married," Abby muttered. "Never ever ever."

She was about to open the door to her room when she heard Tucker's voice, once again coming from the bathroom. Abby froze. She remembered her talk with Noah, about how confronting Tucker was the best option. But now that she was home and he was here, her usual fear of the fight overcame her. So she needed more information? Well, here was her chance to get some.

"Yes! Yes I'll be there. I can't wait!" Tucker said as

Abby inched toward the door. "No . . . No, Carol doesn't suspect a thing."

Abby squeezed her hands into fists.

"Yes. I'll bring the wine," Tucker said. "See you then."

The cell phone beeped as if it was being shut off and Abby ran back to the steps to fake like she was just coming up the stairs. Tucker opened the door to the bathroom, saw her and paused. He had guilt written all over his face.

"Hi," he said, recovering quickly. She saw him slip his cell into his pocket. He wiped his palms on his pants, as if they were sweaty. Oh, he was so busted! "How's it going?"

"Fine," Abby said.

Just do it! Just call him out! Abby screamed in her head. But she found that she could barely even look him in the eye. As if *she* were the guilty party. What was wrong with her?

"You?" she asked.

"Fine!" he said brightly.

"Great!"

She walked by him into her room and slammed the door, fighting for her breath. Screw talking to Tucker. He was obviously guilty. All she had to do was get tangible proof and this whole wedding thing would be history. Her parents would go back to being normal and Carol could stay home and hopefully get her job back. No more separation anxiety, no more fighting about finger foods.

Abby was going to single-handedly save her

family from self-destructing. All she had to do was figure out how.

Carol and Tucker's Engagement Gifts

Mom and Dad: China set of Carol's choice (TBD)

Tucker's mom: Two cut crystal vases (hideous)

Tucker's dad and stepmom: Two ceramic vases (ultra-hideous)

Great-aunt Peggy: Trifle bowl (Huh?)

Aunt Lori: Sandwich maker (Grilled cheese! Sweet!)

Mr. and Mrs. Luther Cox: Silver tea set (Is this 1789?)

Mr. and Mrs. Mark Brandeis: Silver tea set (Maybe it's a Colorado thing.)

Mr. and Mrs. Randy Parker: Silver tea set (Okay, where's the hidden camera?)

Tessa: Leather photo album (She hasn't completely lost her mind.)

Missy: Cut-crystal frame (She has.)

Andrew (Tucker's brother): DVD player (Wait. Was I supposed to get them something???)

· 9 ·

You May Now Kiss the Bride

This is not my life, Abby thought as she slumped down in her desk chair on Sunday afternoon. She crossed her arms over her chest and twisted her mouth into a sour pucker. She didn't even want to think about the scrimmage going on down at the park right now, but her legs would not listen. They bounced up and down maniacally like they knew they were missing out.

Next weekend, Abby thought. *Maybe* next *weekend I'll actually get to play again.*

Carol had typed up the list of songs for Abby to burn on the hundred blank CDs that sat on her floor.

Abby had suggested a few songs that were, oh, recorded in their lifetime, but Carol was adamant. She wanted this to be a CD that all the guests would enjoy. Even Tucker's grandparents.

"How about 'It's the End of the World As We Know It'?" Abby muttered to herself.

Downstairs, a door slammed and Abby flinched. Her parents had been slamming things all morning—doors, cabinets, the occasional window. It was making Abby very tense and very uncomfortable. She was not used to her parents arguing. She wasn't even used to them disagreeing. When were they going to make up?

Slam! Stomp . . . stomp . . . stomp. Slam!

"All right, that's it. I'm out," Abby said to her empty room. She grabbed her bag and keys and headed for the van, her adrenaline pumping. At least there was no Sunday wedding this week. That would have been the icing on the cake.

"Abby!"

She whirled around, her heart in her throat. There was Becky sitting on one of the lattice benches in front of the house, surrounded by papers and magazines. She was uncharacteristically dressed down in jeans and a Boston College sweatshirt, her hair pulled back in a low ponytail. There was no makeup in sight.

"What are you doing here? There's no wedding today," Abby said.

"I know. I'm just . . ." Becky wrung her hands together and looked around at her things.

"Becky? What's wrong?" Abby asked.

"It's . . . your parents," Becky said. "I think they're a little . . . confused."

Tell me about it, Abby thought. "What do you mean?" she asked, sitting down next to Becky.

"Well, they keep giving me things to do for Carol's wedding and at first I was psyched, you know, to have the responsibility? But now—well, just look."

Becky handed Abby a few papers. As Abby looked them over, her stomach twisted into tighter and tighter knots. In her dad's handwriting was a note to call Candyland and Candy Corner to price out various candy stands. There was a page from *Brides* magazine showing a flavored tea station, with a Post-it attached. On it her mom had written, "Love this!" Her dad had written a list of flowers to order—all red roses and gerbera daisies and other crimson varieties. Her mother had given Becky a list of whites—orchids, lilies and the like.

"It's like they're not even talking to each other about what they're giving me," Becky said hopelessly. "What am I supposed to do with all this?"

Abby sighed and leaned back. Becky had hit the nail right on the head—her parents weren't talking to each other. Unless making banging noises counted as talking, which it didn't.

"Becky, listen, it's Sunday. Just . . . go home, put all of this in a drawer or something and relax," Abby told her. "Don't let my insane parents stress you out. We'll figure out a plan. I swear."

Becky's whole face brightened and she grabbed

Abby into a hug. "Thank you!" she said. "Thank you so much! I was starting to think I was just going to have to quit or something."

"No! Don't do that!" Abby blurted out, pulling back. If Becky quit, her parents would be left high and dry—especially if she made it to Italy next year. "We'll talk about it next week, okay? In the meantime, just keep yessing both of them. Got it?"

"Got it," Becky said with a smile.

It looked like someone was going to have to take charge of this wedding before it got completely out of hand. Unfortunately Abby seemed like the only one sane enough to do it.

• • •

I can't believe I'm doing this, Abby thought as she pulled the van onto Main Street. *I've become one of those freaky stalker girls.*

Instead of heading for Van Merck as Abby had originally intended, she found herself making her way downtown toward the bakery. She paused at the stop sign diagonally across from Spencer's. There were a couple of cars in the strip mall parking lot, but most of the stores had already closed. A few of the fluorescent lights in the ceiling were still lit, casting a dim glow over the huge wedding cake in the window. A shadow crossed in front of the door and Abby held her breath.

"It's probably just Mr. Spencer," she told herself, breathing deeply to calm her pounding heart.

Just then the lights inside flicked off and the front door of the bakery opened. Out walked Noah and two

144

other guys, all wearing Red Sox paraphernalia. Abby felt a sudden panic. If Noah saw her she'd look like such a stalker. But there was no way they weren't going to see her. Her big, white, marshmallow van was just too much of an eyesore.

She was just getting ready to make a sharp right when at that very moment a car horn honked long and loud. Abby glanced in the rearview mirror. There was a truck idling behind her and the red-faced driver was making some unsavory gestures in her direction. Her eyes darted toward the bakery and Noah looked right at her. He smiled and waved and Abby now had no choice. She made a left into the parking lot, braking to the soundtrack of shouting and swearing from the truck driver.

Shakily, Abby put the van into park as Noah walked over to her window. She rolled it down.

"Wow. That guy was not happy," Noah said, leaning his arms on her windowsill. He looked ridiculously cute in his faded jeans, white Red Sox jersey and backward baseball cap. A few shocks of dark hair curled up around the band and were flattened down behind his ears.

"I think I could take him," Abby joked back.

"So . . . what're you doing here?" Noah asked. "I know you didn't stop by to see me."

Abby's heart thumped. Was she imagining it or was there something semihopeful in his eyes? Like maybe he was *hoping* she was stopping by just to see him. Abby glanced over at his friends, who were loitering by a Jeep Cherokee, watching her.

"I—uh—I left my jacket at the store this morning," she lied. "I just came back for it."

"Oh . . . well, are you doing anything right now?" Noah asked.

"No!" Abby answered, instantly regretting how overexcited she sounded.

Noah smiled and leaned a little closer to the door—a little closer to her. Was he flirting? It felt to Abby like he might be flirting. Either that or she was just imagining it because all she could think about was grabbing him and kissing him.

"Cuz we have an extra ticket for the Red Sox game," he said. "You want to come?"

"They're playing the Yankees," Abby said, her jaw dropping slightly. "They're playing the Yankees and you have an extra ticket and you want me to come? What happened to the guy with the other ticket? Did he get hit by a bus or something?"

"I take that as a yes," Noah said with a laugh. He opened her van door.

"Hell yeah, it's a yes." Abby grabbed her keys, hopped out and locked the van. "How the heck do you have an extra ticket to a Red Sox–Yankees game?" she asked as she headed for the SUV. Already she was pulling out her cell to call home and tell them not to expect her for dinner. Not that anyone would even notice.

And I get to avoid it for a whole night! Abby thought. To go to a Red Sox–Yankees game with Noah, no less. Noah who just might have been flirting with her. Driving into town was the best move she had ever made.

"Don't you want to go get your jacket?" Noah asked, behind her.

Abby turned around. He was still standing by the front of the van, his shoulder turned toward Sports Expert. Abby noticed that Barb had already turned the front lights off. She was sure her boss was still in the back, going over inventory, but Noah didn't need to know that.

"Oh! I totally spaced. Barb already went home," she said, adding a laugh for effect.

Noah just gave her a look. A look that told her he didn't believe a word she was saying.

"You're certifiable, you know that don't you?"

"Yeah," Abby replied, her cheeks flushing crimson. "I'm aware."

• • •

"Let's go, Sox! Let's go, Sox! Let's go, Sox!"

Abby chanted happily as she looked out the window of Ryan's Cherokee. It had been an awesome game. The Red Sox had kicked Yankee butt, winning 12–3 and shutting down what could have been an eighth-inning comeback with a killer double play. Abby, Noah, and his friends Ryan and Dakar had been cheering and chanting all the way home.

"This girl is good luck," Dakar said. "We should take her to all the games. Screw Alex."

"Yeah, screw Alex!" Ryan agreed. They drove by a car with a Red Sox flag attached to its window and Ryan honked the horn. The kids in the backseat shouted and waved.

"I'm all for it," Abby said. "What do we have to do to make this Alex guy disappear?"

"Shouldn't be a problem," Ryan said, glancing in the rearview. "He missed today because he was ball-and-chaining it. A few more weeks with that girl and he'll be fully housebroken."

"Whipped, huh?" Abby said.

"Totally," Dakar replied.

"Come on, guys. Emma's not that bad," Noah said, smiling at Abby.

"Not that bad!" Dakar and Ryan said in unison.

"She threw out *all of his Red Sox gear,*" Dakar cried.

"And makes him wear *pastel-colored polo shirts!*" Ryan piped in.

"My God, man. Maybe you need to be replaced, too!" Dakar added, laughing.

"I just like to rile them up," Noah whispered to Abby.

Abby laughed and looked out the window again. The game had been exactly what she needed. Shouting at the top of her lungs, eating plenty of junk food, spending quality time with not only Noah, but with two guys who probably hated weddings as much as she did. It was a perfect night.

"Well, here you go," Ryan said, pulling into the strip mall parking lot. He turned around in his seat and offered his hand. "Abby, it was a pleasure."

"Thanks," Abby said, shaking his hand.

"Until next time," Dakar said.

"Thanks for driving, Ry," Noah said, climbing out of the car. He knocked fists with Ryan through the open window and then the Cherokee drove away. They stood there for a moment in silence and finally Abby sighed. She definitely didn't want this night to end.

"They loved you, you know," Noah said, looking down at her.

"I could tell," Abby replied.

She turned and walked slowly toward the van. "I had an amazing time," she said. "Thank you."

"Anytime." He paused in front of the bakery window and Abby turned to face him.

"What?"

"We should do it again sometime," he said, his hands in his pockets.

"Definitely."

"I mean . . . without my stupid friends."

"They're not stupid," Abby replied quickly. "They–"

Noah took a step closer to her and Abby shut up. There it was again. That insane sizzle of attraction. Only this time it was about triple the intensity. Like if Abby reached out and touched the air between them her hand would get singed. Noah's blue eyes stared into hers. For once his lips weren't twisted into a teasing smile or a superior smirk. He was just . . . looking at her.

"Let's not talk about them anymore," he said.

"'Kay" was all Abby could get out.

Noah reached for her, hooked his fingers through the belt loops on the front of her jeans, and pulled her toward him. She tripped on her way and started to laugh out of sheer embarrassment and giddiness. He stopped the laugh with a long, soft, lingering kiss.

Noah Spencer is kissing me! Abby thought, elated. *I'm kissing Noah Spencer!*

Somehow she got past her shock and her arms found their way around his neck. She leaned into him, exhilarated, yet inexplicably comfortable at the same time. It was a totally perfect kiss—mind-numbing and skin-tingling and heart-stopping.

"That was a long time coming," he said softly.

"Really?" Abby asked, floating somewhere above their heads. "How long?"

"Two years, at least."

Abby broke into a wide grin. "Are you kidding? You have not liked me for two years."

Noah smiled. "Is that so hard to believe?"

"Well, yeah, considering how many girlfriends you've had in that time!" Abby replied. "Let's see, there was Courtney, Diana, the unfortunate Brianna incident . . ."

"Someone's been keeping track," Noah joked.

Abby's mind reeled. "So all this time you've been picking on me, messing with me. All this time you've—"

"Wanted to kiss you," Noah said, flushing. "Yeah."

"So why now?" Abby asked.

"I don't know," Noah said with a shrug. "I kind of thought you were flirting with me tonight."

"Me? Flirting?" Abby protested. "I don't even know how!"

Noah laughed. "Well, I figured after all this time it was about time I took a chance."

Abby rested her cheek on his chest and looked up at him. "Well, I'm glad you did," she said. Then she smiled as he leaned in to kiss her again.

This time, without the element of surprise, she was able to take the whole thing in—his soft lips, his fingertips on her face—and she smiled behind her kisses. Noah tasted like ballpark pretzels and mustard. It was Abby's new favorite flavor.

• • •

Abby was back home, but she wasn't ready to rejoin her crazy family. Not just yet. She wanted to hold on to this perfect feeling just a little longer—this feeling of euphoria and expectation, of excitement and weightlessness. She walked around the side of the Dove's Roost and into the backyard. The crickets were chirping and there was a faint breeze rustling the trees.

Abby noticed that the flower-covered canopy her father had created for the wedding the day before had yet to be broken down. Abby stood under the white arch and looked up at the pink and purple flowers that dripped from the sides. She let out a long, happy sigh that dissolved into a laugh.

All her life, she'd always thought the canopy was totally cheesy with the fake-vine inlay on the poles and the little doves carved out near the top. But now . . . now as she grinned in the moonlight and leaned back against one of the supports to look up into the blanket of flowers, she had to admit it.

The canopy was actually kind of pretty.

· 10 ·

One True Love

"You and Cakeboy? I knew it!" Christopher cried, turning his Honda onto Maple Avenue. "I'm, like, a chick, yo. That's how intuitive I am."

"Okay, I'm going to pretend you didn't just say that," Abby said.

"No, but really, I'm happy for you guys," Christopher told her. "And maybe now he'll stop being such a jerk all the time."

Christopher pulled his car up in front of Petals-n-Stems, the flower shop Carol had chosen for her wedding.

"Thanks for the ride," Abby said. "Once this wedding's over I'll actually get full use of the van back."

"Anytime," Christopher said. "We're gonna miss you on the field today."

"Thanks," Abby said. "I'm gonna miss me on the field too." She glanced up as she unbuckled her seat belt and saw that Carol was standing outside the shop talking to Noah. He turned around and smiled and Abby's heart responded even more enthusiastically than usual. It had validation now! Its feelings were reciprocated!

"Aw, look. There's your luv-ah now!" Christopher said.

"Shut up!" Abby cried, smacking his arm.

"Hey!" Noah said, coming over to the window.

"Hi!" Abby replied with a grin. *Please, please don't let Christopher say anything stupid.*

"Carol asked me to sit in on the meeting," Noah explained. "We work with these guys a lot and it's good to coordinate the cake with the flowers."

"Right," Abby said.

Noah looked past her at Christopher. "Hey, man," he said.

"'Sup?" Christopher replied.

"Thanks again, Christopher," Abby said as Noah opened the car door for her. "Call you later."

Christopher cranked up the hip-hop CD in his stereo and peeled out.

"So, you and Johnny Rockets spend a lot of time together, huh?" Noah said.

He's jealous! Abby thought, a thrill of excitement running though her.

"You know we do," she said. "And you also know Christopher and I are just friends."

"It's impossible for guys and girls to just be friends," Noah said.

"Why does everyone keep saying that?" Abby replied. "Besides, *we* were."

Noah grinned. "Yeah, and look how that turned out."

Carol flipped her cell phone closed and looked up. "Hey, Ab. That was Tessa. She said she and Missy are coming over tonight to try working on the shower again. You up for it?"

"I'm not going to go all *Exorcist* again, I promise," Abby said. "I even set the meeting up myself."

"Wow." Carol looked impressed. "That's great. Thanks."

"Just trying to be a good little maid of honor," Abby replied.

"You went all *Exorcist*?" Noah asked.

"Don't worry. My head only spins around when I'm provoked," Abby said, waggling her eyebrows.

"Okay. Let's go look at some flowers," Carol said.

"Cool," Abby replied. "So where's Tucker?"

"Oh, he stayed home to help Dad with the seating arrangements. He said flowers are not a guy thing," Carol said. "No offense, Noah."

"None taken."

Abby shot Noah a look as they followed Carol into the flower shop.

"I know what you're thinking and just because the guy doesn't have an opinion on flowers, that doesn't make him a bad person," Noah whispered to her.

"Yeah," Abby said. "We'll see."

"So . . . I have nothing to worry about with Johnny Rockets?" Noah asked. He glanced over his shoulder as if Christopher and his car were still there.

As Carol greeted Liam, the proprietor of Petals-n-Stems, Abby looked at Noah. His eyes studied hers intently as he waited for an answer and Abby's stomach filled with dancing butterflies. Wow. Noah was really cute when he was threatened. And it was so sweet the way he was so willing to wear his heart on his sleeve.

Initiating physical contact had never been Abby's thing, but on impulse, she reached out and squeezed his hand. Noah smiled.

"Nope," Abby said. "Nothing at all."

• • •

Abby sighed and dropped the spaghetti straps she was struggling with. She needed a moment to catch her breath. Cardio-dress-trying-on. At this rate she was going to be able to teach the class.

What was I thinking saying I wanted to shop for my own dress? she wondered, staring at herself in the dressing room mirror. *At least if I had agreed to the plaid I wouldn't have had to spend my first Friday off from school trying stuff on at Monique's.*

"Everything okay in there?" Carol asked from outside the door.

"I'm fine," Abby replied. "I just can't figure out how these straps go."

"Here. Let me see."

The door to the dressing room opened and the saleswoman, a big-haired chick with a pinched face who was about Carol's age, stood in the doorway. She looked Abby up and down, amused. A couple of women strolled by and peered in at Abby's half-naked body.

"Would you mind closing the door?" Abby asked.

"You have it on backward," the woman told Abby. She put her hand over her mouth and shook her head like it was just *so sad* that Abby was so clueless. Didn't these people work on commission? Shouldn't this woman try being *nice* to Abby?

Carol's face appeared over the woman's shoulder. Abby shot her a pleading look.

"Forget that one," Carol said, glancing at the fabric bunched up all around Abby's waist. "It's not you."

"Thank you," Abby said, shoving the dress to the floor.

She grabbed the door away from the saleswoman, slamming it shut. Three dresses down, two to go. At least Carol had agreed to let Abby get a regular dress from a regular store instead of going to one of those shops that sold nothing but bridesmaids' dresses, most of which looked like wardrobe from an '80s prom movie. At Monique's they had a few normal dresses—i.e., clothes Abby might be caught dead in.

Abby looked at herself in the mirror. Thank God it was Friday. This week she had already had two meetings with Tessa and Missy to pick out color schemes and hors d'oeuvres for the shower. Then she'd addressed, stuffed and mailed the invites and taken the first few RSVPs. And now the week of wedding mayhem was being topped off by this. At least when it was over she had something to look forward to. Noah was picking her up from the dress shop in less than an hour to take her out on their first real date. His friends were having an end-of-the-school-year party and Noah had invited her to go.

"Which one are you trying on now?" her sister asked.

"The light blue one," Abby replied. She stepped out to show Carol. "What do you think?" she said, giving a twirl. It felt slightly itchy, and the neckline was all wrong, but she was trying to give it the benefit of the doubt. "Is it that bad?" she said, taking in Carol's glum expression.

"Please. It's not that," Carol said. She looked up at Abby and for the first time Abby noticed the big bags under her eyes. "Aren't you worried about Mom and Dad?"

Abby chewed her bottom lip. Of course she was worried. Over the past few days her parents hadn't just stopped talking about wedding-related matters. They'd stopped talking entirely. Abby had been hoping things would just somehow go back to normal. She'd been trying to convince herself that maybe it was no big deal. But the fact that Carol was bringing it up made the whole thing feel a lot more real.

"Don't worry," Abby said, trying to sound comforting. "Once the wedding is over everything will go back to normal."

"That's just it," Carol said. "Ab, this is my wedding. I'd rather things go back to normal *before* I walk down the aisle. I don't want Mom and Dad fighting on my wedding day."

Abby swallowed hard and stepped back into the dressing room, her pulse pounding in her ears as she searched for the right words.

"I know it's bad timing," she said as she unzipped the dress and let it fall down around her ankles. "But they'll work it out. It'll be fine." Maybe if she said it enough, she could convince herself too.

"Yeah," Carol said unenthusiastically. "You're probably right."

Abby pulled the last dress off the hanger and slipped her arms through the sheer cap sleeves. She zipped it up and stepped out.

Carol immediately sat up straight. "Wow," she said. "*That* looks good."

"Yeah?" Abby asked, feeling a little thrill of excitement.

She turned around and checked herself out in the mirror. The color was a bit more purply than she would have preferred, but the style flattered her shoulders and the length, just below the knee, was just where she wanted it. There was a lighter-colored ribbon around the waist that on the hanger looked cheesy, but on her person looked much better. It wasn't the most perfect dress she'd ever seen, but Carol seemed to like it. And at that moment, Abby felt like doing something to cheer her sister up.

"Abby, you look really beautiful in that," her sister said, standing up behind her.

"Great! We have a winner!"

At that moment the saleswoman scurried over and glanced at Abby. "That dress was totally made for you."

"You don't have to give us your spiel," Carol told her with a smile. "We already decided to take it."

"Good choice," the woman said flatly. "Just tell them at the register that Annabelle helped you."

"Commission does horrible things to people," Abby said as the woman moved away again.

She and Carol both laughed. Just then the door opened. Noah walked in and Abby froze, her heart pounding. She wanted to dive back into the dressing room so she could change back before he'd see her. But it was too late. Noah found them with his eyes, then made a face that no one had ever made before while looking at Abby. He was stunned.

"Uh . . . hi," Abby said.

"Wow," Noah said. He ran his hand over his hair and pressed his lips together. "You're gonna get that one, right? You look . . . good."

Blushing, Abby ducked into her little closet and slapped her hand over her mouth to stifle the gleeful laugh that had bubbled up in her chest. Apparently they had picked the right dress. Maybe being a bridesmaid wouldn't be so bad after all.

• • •

Abby stood on the deck at Michael Randall's house, smiling shyly at the people around her. She didn't know many of Noah's friends, and barely recognized anyone at this party, which was good and bad. Good because she wasn't forced to make small talk. Bad because she felt totally out of place. Abby had attended the public school in Watertown up until eighth grade, so she recognized a few faces, but this was a graduation party. The few people who looked vaguely familiar were Noah's age, two years ahead of her.

She leaned against the railing on the deck and looked out over the huge backyard. Directly below her were a pool and patio where a few people milled around talking, drinking and smoking.

Below the pool the backyard sloped down into a field where a volleyball net was set up. A bunch of kids were lazily punching a ball back and forth. Trees lined the yard on all sides and vines and bushes nearly camouflaged an old wooden fence.

This would be a pretty place for a wedding, Abby thought. She could picture Carol walking down the deck steps and along the side of the patio to an arch set up where the volleyball court now was. She smiled slightly, then caught herself and rolled her eyes.

Since when did her brain do *that*?

"Finally found the soda," Noah said, reaching around her to hand her a plastic cup. "You'd think all Michael's family drinks is beer. The whole refrigerator is full of it."

"Well, it *is* a party," Abby joked.

She clicked her cup with Noah's and took a sip. Down below a couple of guys chased a miniskirted girl with a supersoaker water gun. She screeched and protested as they blasted her white T-shirt until everyone could see the flowered lace of her bra right through the fabric.

"You guys!" the girl whined, smiling all the way. "This is a party! Not a wet T-shirt contest!"

"It is now!" one of the guys said, dousing another girl as she passed.

"Wow. There is some great people-watching at this party," Abby said. *Note to self: steer clear of those particular Neanderthals.*

"Yeah. There are some people I am not going to miss," Noah said. He sipped at his soda and looked down. His face grew serious as the party raged around them.

"Did you—I mean—did you want to go away to school?" Abby hoped her asking didn't seem weird. She didn't want him to think she was presuming anything.

"Nah." Noah placed his soda aside and shrugged. "I mean, not that I don't want to see the world . . . I do. All of it. But for now I need to help my dad out. And I can take a few classes at RCC and maybe find out what I'm really interested in."

"You don't know yet?" Abby asked.

"No. You?" Noah asked.

"I'm thinking about being a nuclear physicist," Abby joked. "Or maybe an eyebrow plucker. I hear you can make a killing in New York."

Noah laughed. "Somehow I don't see you as the plucking type."

"I live to pluck," Abby deadpanned.

They turned back to watch the scenes playing out on the vast yard below. "If your dad really needs the help, why don't you guys just hire a manager and a delivery person?" Abby rested her elbows on the railing. "It's not like you can't afford it. I know how much those cakes cost," she added with a narrowing of her eyes.

Noah smirked. "Yeah, we probably could. But this business means a lot to my dad. And he's always been there for me. I mean, he raised me by himself after my mom died and he taught me everything he knows. Besides, I really *enjoy* the work, so for now I think I'll just stick close to home."

Abby looked at him and he smiled again. Here she was, trying to do everything she could just to get away from the Roost for a year, and here Noah was putting college on hold to stay home with his dad. How would it feel to really *want* to be at the Dove's Roost? To *crave* a life of menu building, ribbon tying and place setting?

Abby let out a long sigh. If only she could get psyched about the weekly nuptials, she wouldn't have to desert her family. She could stay home next year and be the model employee.

And besides . . . Noah was going to be here. The distance between Italy and Massachusetts would be a tough one to conquer even for a person who *had* experience with relationships.

It was definitely something to think about.

• • •

The stream that burbled through the center of Van Merck Park had never seemed like much to Abby.

She'd kicked one of her favorite red Keds into it when she was in first grade and a Canadian goose had grabbed it and run off. That was about the only interesting thing that had ever happened in this spot. Up until now anyway. Tonight she was seeing the stream in a whole new way. With the dim streetlights flickering a few dozen yards away and the stars blazing overhead—with a couple of open Chinese food containers and not another soul in sight except for Noah Spencer—it was actually really romantic.

"Try the shrimp. It's intense," Noah said, spearing a piece with his fork.

He held it out to her, but Abby wasn't exactly at the mushy feeding-each-other stage yet. In fact she hoped to never be at that icky stage with anyone ever in her life. Instead she grabbed the fork from his hand and plucked the shrimp off between her teeth.

"Jimmy's is the best Chinese food I've ever tasted," she said.

Noah laughed. "I bet it's the only Chinese food you've ever tasted."

Abby frowned. "Well, Jimmy's *is* the only place in town, but there's a reason," she said. "No one's stupid enough to try to compete with him."

"Point taken," Noah said. "You know, I think we got out of that party just in time. Ryan was about to suggest a game of strip water polo."

"They would have had to kill me dead to get me to participate," Abby said, taking a sip of her soda.

"Yeah, and I don't think your dad would appreciate my bringing home nothing but your cold, stiff body."

Abby laughed. "Probably not."

They sat in silence for a moment, smiling and eating. It was so quiet and relaxed Abby almost forgot about what a war zone her life had become. Out here with Noah, it felt like peacetime.

"This is nice," Noah said finally.

"What is?"

"This. Hanging out with you."

"We hang out all the time," Abby said. But she flushed nonetheless.

"I know . . . but this is different," Noah said. "It is, isn't it?"

Abby smiled. She knew exactly what he meant. It was different now because she was always wondering whether he was going to kiss her again. That stomach-clenching feeling of uncertainty and anticipation stayed with her the whole time. She used to hang out with Noah and wonder whether or not he was going to give her a wedgie.

"I have to say something and it's probably gonna freak you out, but remember that if you run, I know where you live," Noah said suddenly.

"Okay," Abby said. She turned toward him.

"Abby." His face was very serious. "I think I'm sort of in love with you."

Abby laughed—loud. She couldn't help it. And she couldn't stop. She put her hand over her mouth and looked at Noah, mortified. Maybe now *he* was going to run.

"Okay, not the reaction I was looking for," Noah said.

"No! No! I'm sorry!" Abby told him. She moved a carton of kung pao chicken out of the way and slid closer to him on the bench. "I'm sorry—that was stupid. It was just a knee-jerk—"

"It's okay, it's cool," Noah said. He was wiping his palms on the thighs of his jeans. Over and over.

"No!" Abby was overheating. "That's not what I mean."

She reached out and grabbed him by his cheeks with her thumb and forefinger. His mouth smushed into a pucker. It was ridiculous, but it was the only thing she could think to do to get him to look at her.

And then she opened her mouth and blurted it out, before she could let herself doublethink how it would sound. "I love you, too!"

Noah's eyes lit up.

"Rearry?" he said, his face still squashed in her hand.

Abby finally let him go.

"Yes, really," she said. "I know it feels fast, but—"

"But it's not," Noah finished for her. "Because we've known each other—"

"Forever," she said.

They both laughed at the silliness of the moment, then Noah reached over and placed his hand on hers. Abby moved closer to him.

"I'm gonna kiss you now," Noah said, looking deep into her eyes.

"You'd better," Abby said.

• • •

By the time Abby got home the only lights on were in the catering kitchen and the ballroom, where the workers were cleaning up after that night's event. Abby approached the house, giggling at nothing. She let herself into the residence, walked into the kitchen and paused. There, in the dim light from the overhead stove lamp, were Carol and Tucker, making out. Right in the middle of the room. Tongues and all.

Abby slammed the door to let them know she was there. They broke the lip contact and turned to look at her, but didn't even have the decency to fly apart in embarrassment.

"Hey, Ab! I'm glad you're here," Carol said. "We were just trying to figure out how to do our first kiss at the ceremony."

Abby grimaced. "Not like that," she said. "Unless you're sending your wedding video in as a porn audition tape."

Tucker laughed and wiped his mouth with the back of his hand. "Yeah. Guess we got a little carried away."

Ew. I so don't need the details, Abby thought.

"Okay, so what do you think of this?" Carol asked, moving toward Tucker again, all puckered and ready to go.

"Wait a minute, wait a minute, wait a minute," Abby said, waving a hand in front of her face. "You want me to help you pick out a *kiss?*"

"Yeah," Carol said with a shrug. "It's important, Abby. Now watch."

Ewewewewew! This is not *happening!* Abby thought.

Carol slipped her arms around Tucker's neck and gave him a long, mercifully closed-mouthed smooch.

"What do you think?" Carol asked. "Does it look all right?" She sounded like someone who was trying on a pair of shoes.

"Perfect," Abby said, moving toward the stairs. "Perfect. Wouldn't change a thing."

"Wait! You didn't see the other one!" Carol called after her.

But Abby was already halfway up the stairs. This whole thing was definitely out of hand.

Abby slipped into her room and closed the door behind her. She closed her eyes tight and tried to recapture the moment between her and Noah. Her face felt tight and tingly from making out with him and when she heard his voice in her head, telling her he loved her, her entire chest filled with a blissful warmth. She breathed in deep and let it out slowly, a smile playing about her lips. There. That was better.

Kicking off her shoes, Abby headed for her bed, where she planned on flopping down, falling right to sleep and dreaming about kissing Noah all night.

When she hit her bed something crunched beneath her. Abby rolled over, half expecting to find a list of bridesmaid duties for tomorrow, but instead was greeted with a pile of mail. A flyer from Lockport about another successful school year—they loved to advertise themselves. A couple of catalogs—Title Nine Sportswear and Urban Outfitters. And a thick brown packet from . . . Student XChange.

Abby gulped, feeling a sudden mix of excitement and confusion. Where had this come from? Who had gotten the mail? Had her parents seen the return address and figured out what she'd done?

She tore open the end of the packet with her finger. She tipped the gnarled envelope on its side and let its contents tumble onto the bed. There was the glossy catalog Christopher had showed her. A few folded papers of different colors and sizes and . . . one letter on cream-colored stationery.

Abby unfolded the letter with shaking fingers. She held her breath and read.

Dear Ms. Beaumont,
   We are pleased to inform you that you have been accepted into the Student XChange program for Lockport Academy for the next academic year with full scholarship funding (see enclosed financial aid materials).

"Oh . . . my . . . God!" Abby said under her breath. She'd gotten in! She'd really gotten in! Abby Beaumont was going to Italy! She rolled over on her bed and reached for her phone to call Delila and tell her the good news, still clutching the letter in her free hand. She was halfway through her best friend's phone number when she stopped cold.

Yes, she was going to Italy with Delila and Christopher. And she would be leaving Noah behind.

Abby blew out a breath and flopped onto her back.

"Oh . . . crap."

Engagement Gifts, continued . . .

Mr. and Mrs. Paul Condon: Ice cream maker (Can you say pointless?)

Mr. and Mrs. Barry Ring: Bread maker (That's direct-to-attic gift buying.)

Ms. Celia Malloy: Quesadilla maker (Now this is an appliance I can get behind.)

Mr. Richard Gill: Plastic-bag sealer (Because . . . ?)

Mr. and Mrs. Leon Kapusta: Cedar-, birch- and pine-scented candle set. (And who doesn't love the smell of wood?)

Mr. and Mrs. Drew Bartholomew: ??? (Not sure what this thing is. Paperweight? Wall decoration? Simple dust magnet? It looks like a heart, maybe? An abstract crystal heart paperweight? Just what every couple starting out really needs!)

· 11 ·

In Sickness and in Health

Abby leaned her elbows on the wooden countertop and stared out the window at the traffic passing by. It was drizzling outside and the hiss of the tires running through the rain was lulling her into a near coma state.

I'm going to Italy, Abby thought. She rested her chin in her hands and repeated it again in her head. *I'm going to Italy . . . if I ever tell my parents about it and they let me go and I actually decide I* want *to go. . . .*

"Wednesdays are kind of boring around here, huh?" Barb said, leaning in next to Abby.

"I'm sorry," Abby replied, standing up straight. "Do you need me to do something?"

"Tell me what's up," Barb said, raking her fingers through her short white hair. "You've been dazed and confused all week."

Abby's face flushed and she looked at the floor. "Sorry," she said. "There's just a lot going on right now."

"Anything you want to talk about?" Barb asked. "It's got to be more interesting than sorting the sock bin."

Normally Abby was not the talking-about-it type, but Barb really seemed concerned. And she needed to talk to someone. . . .

"Okay, well, I have something huge I have to ask my parents, but they kind of have other things on their minds right now," Abby said.

"Like your sister's wedding?" Barb asked.

"Basically." Abby pulled the canister of sports-themed pencils toward her on the desk and ran her hand over the erasers. No reason to bring up the constant fighting that was going on.

"What's the something huge? If you don't mind my asking."

Abby stopped fidgeting and looked at Barb. "I got into a student exchange program and I'm going to go to Italy for a whole year and play soccer with Roberto Viola." It was the first time she'd said it out loud.

Barb's blue eyes widened and she whistled. "Wow. That *is* big. Congratulations. That Roberto Viola's a hot one."

"Barb! Ew!" Abby exclaimed.

"What? I still got a libido!" Barb replied.

"All right, all right," Abby said, trying to get the mental image of Barb and Roberto Viola out of her head before it stuck there. "So what should I do?"

"You should tell them," Barb said. "They may be all wrapped up in Carol right now, but you're still their daughter and they love you. They should hear about this."

Abby took a deep breath and let it out slowly. Barb was right about one thing—she knew her parents loved her. But she wasn't exactly sure they were going to want to hear about Italy. Especially not with the War of the Wedding being waged at all hours. Abby hadn't even had a chance to tell them about her and Noah yet. Every time she saw them they were both in such horrid moods, she knew they wouldn't react in the ecstatic way she wanted them to. It broke her heart to imagine saying, "Mom! Guess what? I'm totally in love with Noah Spencer!" And her mother looking back at her with that angry determined look on her face, "Don't you think an English garden theme is a beautiful idea? Good. Tell your father."

So instead, Noah was yet another secret.

"Tell them you need them both for half an hour, then sit them down and spill the beans," Barb suggested. "Why not do it this weekend?"

"I can't. Carol's shower is this Sunday," Abby replied. "And I have to make this huge vat of rice pudding."

"Rice pudding?"

"Yeah, it's Carol's favorite. It's for the shower. I've been working on the shower all week and I really want it to be perfect."

Whoa. Was that me who just said that? Abby thought, nearly gagging.

Barb smiled. "You're a good sister, kid. So wait till after the shower, but not long after. Meantime, I got an idea." She slapped Abby on the back, then popped open the register drawer and pulled out a few bills. "Why don't you go over to that bakery you love so much and get us some cannoli to celebrate your international adventure?"

"Really? Thanks!" Abby beamed, grabbing the cash. Free snacks *and* a little Noah time. What could be a better mood lifter? "Be right back!" she called as she jogged for the door.

Abby kept under the awnings along the strip mall to avoid getting soaked. She was giddy with anticipation over getting to see Noah. It was like that feeling she got right before her parents brought out her birthday presents and she loved it. She hustled over to the bakery and whipped the door open. Spencer's was even deader than Sports Expert. There wasn't a soul in sight.

"Hello?" Abby called out.

Nothing. She walked behind the counter and over to the kitchen door, where she stopped, her breath completely taken away. Sitting in the middle of the huge wooden worktable was the most beautiful wedding cake she had ever seen. The white icing was covered with intricate swirls of the lightest light pink and dotted all over the cake were hundreds of tiny, color-ful butterflies. It wasn't just a cake. It was art.

But it wasn't just the cake that left Abby fighting for breath. It was watching Noah, his backward base-ball cap streaked with icing, his brow furrowed in concentration, as he decorated it. He was so intensely focused, he had yet to notice her standing there.

"Wow," she said finally, because she had to say something.

Noah started and looked up. He saw Abby and took a couple of instinctive steps back from the cake.

"Noah! I didn't know you decorated!" Abby said, walking up to get a closer look. "This cake is unbe-lievable."

"Okay, you need to go." Noah grabbed Abby's shoulders and turned her back in the direction from which she'd come. "You were never here. You never saw this. Buh-bye."

"Noah!" Abby said, freeing herself from his grip. "What's your deal?"

"Abby, if my dad found out that you knew I was decorating . . . I think he'd pretty much have a heart attack," Noah said, walking out into the shop.

Abby followed, confused. "What—he doesn't know? How could he not know?"

"It's not that he doesn't know," Noah said. "It's that no one else can know."

"Okay, ya lost me," Abby told him. She leaned back on the bakery case and crossed her arms over her chest, waiting for an explanation.

Noah sucked in a deep breath, put his hands on

his hips and sighed. His face was streaked with flour and icing. All she wanted to do was grab him and kiss him—which she would have done if he weren't being so weird.

"Look, one of the reasons this place does so well is that everyone is guaranteed a wedding cake personally decorated by the famous Dominic Spencer," Noah said, his expression pained. "If it got out that I'd been decorating all the cakes for the last year, it'd be—"

"The last *year*?" Abby exclaimed. "All those cakes you brought over . . . ? You decorated them?"

Noah swallowed. "Yeah."

"Omigod, Noah," Abby said, pushing away from the case. "Some of those cakes were . . . I mean they're gorgeous. You're really good."

Noah smiled for the first time all afternoon. "I know," he said with a laugh. "Sucks, doesn't it?"

"What do you mean?" Abby asked, baffled.

"It's just . . . I'm in this now. For life," Noah said. "This is why I can't go away to school, Ab. I've only been doing this because . . . well, because my dad has serious debilitating arthritis. And it's only getting worse. I'm doing it because he can't."

Abby couldn't believe it. Dominic had arthritis? That would be like Pedro Martinez breaking his pitching arm. Around this town, Dominic was a legend. He must have been heartbroken. And to know the father and son had been dealing with this for a year . . . Abby wasn't quite sure what to say. It was devastating. She looked at Noah, and tilted her head.

"Don't get me wrong. I love decorating," Noah said. "Never thought I would, but it's kind of cool." He smiled and looked back toward the kitchen. "And like you said, I'm pretty good at it."

"Well . . . that's good, then," Abby said.

"Yeah," Noah replied. "And now you know my deepest darkest secret," he said, stepping toward her and putting his arms around her waist. "Just don't tell anyone, okay?"

"I promise," Abby said. She was touched that he'd told her his big secret, even if he'd already sort of had to. As he wrapped her up in a sugarcoated hug, she felt totally amazing, and completely guilty at the same time.

She knew Noah's deep dark secret, but she was still keeping something from him. There was no doubt about it. She had to figure out what to do about Italy, and she had to do it soon.

•   •   •

"Okay, so we're going with the single orchid centerpieces for the tables, right?" Abby was talking into her cell phone while pacing back and forth along the sidelines at Van Merck.

"Yep. Liam has the delivery set for ten a.m.," Tessa told her.

"All right, everybody! Huddle up!" Matt Fiorello called out from the center of the field.

"Great. Okay. My game's about to start. I gotta go–"

"Wait! Abby! We never discussed the favors," Tessa said. "Missy found this company called Custom

Cookies and they have these amazing cookies shaped like little wedding cakes."

Abby glanced at the field, itching to get out there and play.

"That sounds fine," Abby said.

"We want to bring them over to show you and get your approval," Tessa said.

Abby rolled her eyes. "No. You don't have to do that. Little cake cookies sound . . . great!" she said, hoping her enthusiasm sounded convincing.

"Look, Abby, we want you to be included. We're bringing them by."

"Tessa! I'm at the park! I'm playing soccer! You cannot bring cookies by for my approval!" Abby cried. A couple of the guys chuckled as they walked by.

"Look, I don't want a redo of the dress incident," Tessa said. "Carol said to run everything by you, so we're running it by you. Be there in a few. Bye!"

Abby clicked off the phone and groaned. This wedding was following her everywhere. She plopped down on the bench and relaced her cleats just to have something to do. It looked like she was going to miss out on the first game of the day. Missing things seemed to be the theme lately. Last night she had missed out on going to the movies with Delila in order to stay up way too late making Carol's pudding for the shower. It had taken a full hour just to dish it into crystal bowls to store in the fridge. Then that morning she had spent two hours writing out place cards, and this afternoon was reserved for helping her mom decorate the parlor. A little exercise was exactly what she needed to get her mind off the bridal insanity. But she wasn't going to get it until she had a cookie meeting.

There had to be a special place in heaven reserved for maids of honor.

Christopher's car pulled into the lot and Abby smiled as he jogged over to her. The game had already started so she and Christopher were both out. At least she had somebody to chill with while she waited.

"Hey! I'm so glad you're here," he said, catching his breath. He dropped onto the bench and started yanking cleats and shin guards from his bag. "I have to tell you something so cool!"

"What's up?"

"My dad got us press passes for a Revolution game the Wednesday after next," Christopher said proudly. "All access. That means we can be on the sidelines, in the locker room, wherever."

"Whoa. Wait a minute. You mean we're going to get to meet Taylor Twellman and Steve Ralston and actually, like, *talk* to them?"

"The whole team," Christopher said. "*All* access!"

"Omigod!" Abby said, turning sideways on the bench. "This is so amazing! Your dad is my hero! I can't even tell you how much I love you right now."

"Oooh. How would Cakeboy feel about that?" Christopher asked.

"Shut up," Abby replied, flushing.

But Christopher made a good point. How *would*

Noah feel about her and Christopher going off and doing something this cool together? Together alone. He would probably be jealous, she knew. Boys could be so fragile.

I can't tell him, she realized, her stomach turning. If Noah knew about this he'd get suspicious and if he got suspicious things would get tense between them. The last thing Abby needed right now was more complications in her life. *But there won't be any more complications if I don't tell him,* Abby realized.

"Um, Ab? Are those girls over there waving at you?"

Abby looked toward the parking lot to find Tessa and Missy standing by Tessa's car, indeed waving frantically in her direction. Tessa was holding up a cookie and pointing to it while Missy gabbed on her phone.

"I'll be right back," Abby said, jumping up and racing toward them before anyone else noticed. If she knew anything about her soccer buddies it was that they would never let her live down a scene like this.

• • •

Abby walked into the catering kitchen on Sunday morning, all decked out in her maid of honor outfit—a pair of unwrinkled chinos and a blue T-shirt. As soon as she stepped into the room she heard Noah's van pull up out back, and her heart executed a somersault. She rushed over to the door.

"What are you doing here?" she asked.

Noah squeezed her shoulders, then planted a

quick kiss on her lips. Followed by a longer one like he just couldn't resist. Abby had to hold her breath to keep from giggling.

"I came to wish you luck with the shower," Noah said, walking past her into the kitchen.

"Thanks," Abby said.

"And to invite you over for dinner next Wednesday," Noah added.

"Why next Wednesday?" Abby asked, pulling a stack of napkins toward her and starting to fold. *Next Wednesday . . . next Wednesday . . . Why does that sound so familiar?*

"My aunt Ro is coming into town and she's stopping by," Noah said, grabbing a few napkins to help. "She's my mom's sister. You'd love her."

"You want me to meet your aunt?" Abby asked, beaming. It was so sweet!

"Yeah. So, are you free?" Noah asked.

Suddenly it hit her—the reason next Wednesday was stuck in her mind. She was going to the Revolution game with Christopher, which she hadn't told Noah about. Abby swallowed back a lump of acidic guilt. After all, what Noah didn't know couldn't hurt him.

"Actually, I don't know if it's the best idea," she said. "It's only a couple of days before the wedding and I should really be here for Carol, you know, if she needs anything."

Noah's smile faltered, but he nodded. "Wow. You're really starting to take this thing seriously."

"Well, I *am* the maid of honor," Abby joked.

"I understand, but if you're free you can always stop by."

"Yeah," Abby said, relieved. "If I'm free."

"So, I still can't believe you didn't let me make the dessert for this thing," Noah said, leaning against the counter.

"Hey, Carol wanted rice pudding," Abby said, walking over to the fridge and yanking on the door. "And what the bride wants the bride—"

Abby stopped as the horrid stench of sour milk and curdled cream filled her nostrils. Noah took a step back as they both gazed into the refrigerator. The telltale whir of the motor was absent. The light hadn't gone on when she opened the door. The catering fridge had died. And it had taken the rice pudding and all the other food with it.

"Omigod," Abby said. She slammed the door and leaned back against it. "The guests are going to be here in an hour and we have no dessert."

"Don't panic," Noah said. "You happen to have a baker for a boyfriend, remember?"

"But Carol wanted rice pudding. All she talked about the other night for two hours was rice pudding!" She was suddenly seized by panic. "What're we gonna do?"

"Abby, focus," Noah said, stepping forward and putting his hands on her shoulders. "Carol is just going to have to live without the pudding."

"But she's the *bride*!" Abby wailed.

"Ab, I think you've gone over to the dark place," Noah said.

Just then Abby's father stepped into the kitchen. Abby and Noah jumped to attention, standing side by side in front of the fridge. If her father found out the catering fridge was kaput he was going to have a major freak-out and that was not something she could handle right now.

"How's everything going for the shower?" he asked. "Got all the ducks in a row?"

"You bet," Abby said quickly. "Nothing at all to worry about."

"Great. I knew you could handle it, Abby." He planted a quick kiss on her forehead. Then he slipped by them, went out the side door and headed for his office. For once Abby was glad her parents were fighting. Normally her father would have sensed her tension and realized something was up, but at the moment he was too distracted to notice.

"Let's go," Noah said, heading out the door. "You can call Rocco on the way and tell him to get someone to come fix the fridge." He whipped out his cell phone and handed it to her.

"This is never gonna work," Abby said.

"You know what your problem is, Abby?" Noah said as he yanked open the door of his delivery van. "You have no faith."

•   •   •

"Okay, this is never gonna work!" Noah shouted over the loud sloshing of the massive dishwashers at the bakery.

"I told you!" Abby shouted back.

They had walked into Spencer's to find that his father had just sold every last cookie and cupcake to a woman from the Watertown Women's Club who had suddenly at the last second remembered that she'd forgotten to get dessert for a function that afternoon. All that was left in the cases were day-old cakes and a few sorry-looking fruit pies. Noah and Dominic had promised they could whip up six dozen cupcakes in less than forty minutes. As soon as they were done baking, Dominic had retreated to close up the shop, and now Noah and Abby were left trying to decorate seventy-two cupcakes in almost no time.

"Okay, how about this?" Noah said. "You ice and I'll make the flowers."

"Every time I try to ice a cupcake I end up ripping it to shreds," Abby said, looking down at the two already-demolished chocolate blobs in front of her.

"Okay, I'll ice, you do the flowers," Noah said.

Abby just looked at him and blinked. "Noah Spencer, do you know me *at all*?"

"Well, someone's gotta do the flowers!"

"Noah, I know you're an artiste and a perfectionist and all, but it's about time to admit that all we can handle here are sprinkles," Abby said. She glanced at the clock behind his head. "There's just no time."

"Sprinkles? Spencer's Bakery does not do sprinkles for something like this."

"Look, Carol is going to blow a gasket when she realizes I'm gone, if she hasn't already," Abby said firmly. "I have to get out of here."

Noah was still unconvinced. He looked away and pressed his lips together, clearly battling an inner artistic demon. Abby grabbed his chin between her thumb and forefinger and made him look at her.

"What if I promise never to tell anyone the cupcakes came from Spencer's?" she said. "We'll tell them I got 'em at ShopRite."

Noah took an excruciating moment to ponder this, then nodded. "Deal."

"Good," she said. "Now let's sprinkle up these puppies."

Noah grabbed a spatula and a vat of icing and quickly applied it onto the first cupcake, making a perfect swirl in about three seconds. Abby smiled, pulled the cupcake toward her and picked up the shaker of sprinkles. Noah grimaced as she let loose with a huge shower of the colorful pellets.

"See? Pretty!" she said, holding up the cupcake.

Noah shot her a pained look.

"It's gonna be okay," she said, looking at the clock again. "Oh, God. Ten minutes."

After that they worked in silence, icing and sprinkling, icing and sprinkling. Dominic came back from the shop and wordlessly lifted the cupcakes into pink boxes. The three of them were on a mission and before no time the last cupcake was boxed. Abby checked the time.

"It's started," she said.

"You kids get moving," Dominic said, handing over the boxes. "I'll clean up here."

Abby and Noah rushed out the door. Once the boxes were placed safely in the van, Noah slammed it into gear and practically flew across town. By the time they got to the Dove's Roost, dozens of cars were already parked in the lot and the front door was wide open. Noah started to slow the van and Abby's heart hit her throat.

"No! Go to the back! The back!" she hissed, ducking down.

Noah swung the van onto the service driveway and stopped by the catering kitchen door. They jumped out, unloaded the boxes and raced into the house. Noah walked in first and when Abby came up behind him, she froze in her tracks. Carol and her mother were both standing in the center of the kitchen, glaring at her. Rocco hovered next to the refrigerator, his eyes wide. He waved his hands at Abby, then shook his head. The fridge still hadn't been fixed. If Abby had to tell her mother it was dead, and that the thousands of dollars' worth of food that had been in it had gone to waste, Carol wasn't the only person who was going to lose it. And a double Beaumont freak-out was not one of the ingredients in a perfect shower.

It would be over before it ever had a chance to begin.

"Abigail Lynn, what do you think you're doing?" her mother asked. "Do you realize there are forty plus people out there wondering where their hostess is?"

Sheesh! It was like they were living in eighteenth-century England. *Heaven forbid a party should start without the hostess!*

"What are those?" Carol asked, eyeing the pink boxes. "I thought we said rice pudding for dessert."

Abby stopped breathing. Rocco closed his eyes in despair. Noah didn't move a muscle.

"I . . . went another way?" Abby said.

Carol sighed dramatically, walked over to Noah and opened the top box. Abby waited for the meltdown to begin. This was it. All their hard work was for naught.

"Oh, Abby! You remembered!" Carol cried, beaming over at her.

Abby glanced at Noah, confused. "Uh . . ."

"These look exactly like the cupcakes we had at my twelfth birthday party," Carol said, lifting one out. "Only the best birthday party of my *life*!" She walked over to Abby and hugged her around the neck. "You are *so* sweet."

Noah put his boxes down on the counter and collapsed next to them. Abby grinned like she had never grinned before.

"Hey, that's me," she said, breathing for the first time in minutes. "What's a maid of honor for?"

• • •

Abby and Delila stood in the corner of the Dove's Roost's parlor room, watching as Carol's bridal shower went off without a hitch. Carol was in the process of opening yet another box of Waterford crystal. Everyone oohed and aahed. Tessa, who was sitting on the divan to Carol's left, noted the gift and giver on her pink notepad. Missy, on Carol's right, grabbed the ribbon to add to the ribbon bouquet. Carol had insisted that she didn't want the traditional, cheesy ribbon hat, but Missy had just taken that as permission to make an only slightly less offensive clutch version.

"So where's the hottie groom?" Delila asked. She was the only person in the room who had dared wear black to the occasion—a wide-neck T and battered blue jeans.

"Are you kidding? My mother would never let him be in the house for the shower. This is a *female* tradition," Abby said.

"Too bad. I think I had a dream about him last night."

"Delila! Ew!" Abby cried.

"I can't control my subconscious!"

"Well, he's out picking up his brother from the airport," Abby told her. "He's the best man and he's flying in early. Probably to throw some monster bachelor party."

"Oooh! A brother?" Delila said, eyes wide. "Is he staying here, too?"

"No, gutter brain. He's getting a hotel. Let's move on," Abby said.

"All right. Fine. I gotta hand it to ya, kid," Delila said, chomping into a cupcake from her china plate. "The food is killer, and the decorations don't make me want to heave."

"Thanks for the compliment," Abby said with a laugh. "I think everyone's having fun."

"Well, Carol is and that's all that matters," Abby's mother said. She wrapped her arm around Abby's shoulders. "I'm very proud of you, sweetie."

She kissed the side of Abby's head and Abby couldn't help beaming. It was quite a nice little party if she did say so herself. Plus it was good to see her mother calm and smiling. It was the first time in days that the dark cloud had lifted.

You should ask her, a little voice in Abby's mind piped up, sending a thrill of sudden nervousness down her spine. The shower was all but over and who knew when she would see either one of her parents in such a receptive mood again? This could be a now-or-never situation.

But Abby hesitated, her thoughts turning to Noah. Once the cat was out of the bag, there was no turning back. If her parents said yes, she'd be an idiot not to take them up on it and go. But that would mean leaving Noah–the very thought of which made her lose almost all interest in going.

Of course if her parents said no, it would give her the perfect out. It wouldn't be her fault that she wasn't going to Italy. They would be making the decision for her and she'd get to stay home with her new boyfriend . . . and miss out on a potentially life-altering experience.

The whole thing was making her brain hurt.

But it was obviously time to deal. She took a deep breath, steeled herself and turned toward her mother. She had to get this over with before she lost her nerve.

"Phoebe? Can I talk to you for a second?"

The entire room fell silent and every guest looked at the doorway. Abby's father, who had promised to stay in his office for the duration of the shower, was standing there with a cold look on his face. Abby turned toward Carol and saw her own worry reflected in Carol's eyes.

"We're in the middle of Carol's shower," Abby's mother said, visibly tensing.

"I realize that, and I'm sorry, honey," he said, looking toward Carol. "It will only take a moment."

Abby's mother just stood there for a second, frozen. It was clear she was trying to decide between standing up to him and making a scene at her daughter's shower, or kowtowing and doing as he asked. Eventually her protective motherly instincts won out and she started across the room.

"Excuse me for a moment," she said to the guests. As she slipped by Abby's dad, she gave him a look that could have withered an evergreen.

Carol tried to return to her gift opening, but her hands were visibly shaking. Tense voices could be heard coming from the next room. Abby's stomach twisted into a thousand knots and all the guests began to shift uncomfortably. Abby stood up and started for the hallway, somehow thinking that maybe she could defuse the situation. And that's when a door slammed.

"That's it, Phoebe! You have no respect for my opinions," Abby's father shouted loud enough for all to hear.

"David! It was a complete waste of money! If you had any foresight you would see that this pattern is too trendy!" her mother shouted back. "We can't spend tens of thousands of dollars on something that will be collecting dust in our basement come December!"

Abby's father stormed into view on the other side of the door. He whirled to look down the hall at her mom, his face a deep, angry purple. "How dare you cancel an order I placed without even consulting me!"

"How dare you place an order that large without even consulting *me*!"

"That's it. Give me the plate, Phoebe," he said. "I'm calling them back."

"You want the plate? Fine! Here's the plate!"

Suddenly, Abby's father ducked and a piece of china zoomed by the doorway, narrowly missing his head. Abby jumped, her heart hitting her mouth, as the plate crashed against the wall. Everyone in the parlor froze. Carol turned green. Tears welled up in Abby's eyes. Her mother had just thrown a plate at her father. Her mother had just thrown a plate at her father like all the nightmare families that came to the Roost. What was happening to them?

Abby's dad stood. His eyes were still trained down the hall at his wife. "I'll be leaving now," he said shakily.

Abby felt as if someone had just taken a baseball bat to her stomach. She looked at Carol, who had tears in her eyes. No one said a word. All Abby could hear was the sound of her own pulse.

Her dad slammed his way into the residence and stomped upstairs. Everyone was silent and still. A few seconds later Tucker and his brother walked through the front door.

"Hey everyone!" he said happily. "Oh! Are we too early? How's the shower going?"

"Tucker," Abby said, approaching him. "Now really isn't the best time. . . ."

Another door slammed and Carol was on her feet and running across the room in tears.

"Baby? What's wrong?" Tucker asked. He touched her face gently and Abby was instantly grateful to him for being so sweet. Even if it was just for that one moment. And she had no idea what else he was up to.

Carol grabbed Tucker and pulled him out of the room. Abby and Tucker's brother, Andrew, were left all alone at the front of the room facing her aunts, cousins and about a dozen of Carol's friends.

"Um . . . hi," Andrew said.

Delila stepped forward and took his arm. "Are you thirsty? Let me show you where the kitchen is."

Abby shot her friend a grateful look, then turned to the rest of the guests.

And Abby said the first thing that came to mind. "Well, I guess everyone will have a strange story to tell around the dinner table tonight, huh?"

Her mother's sister Lori shot her a sympathetic look, then got up and walked off to find Abby's mother. Becky quickly crossed the room and stood next to Abby.

"Everyone, I think the shower is officially over," Becky said with a businesslike smile. "I'll help you all find your jackets. Thanks for coming."

Becky gave Abby a comforting nod, then moved off to help the guests. Delila returned from the catering kitchen alone. Abby grabbed her into a hug and tried not to cry.

"Don't worry, Ab. They're just stressed," Delila said. "They'll figure it out."

Abby nodded, but she wasn't so sure. She heard the crunch of tires on the drive outside and then the roar of her dad's car's engine. Her parents had never been big fighters and now, they had somehow become plate throwers. How were they going to get through something like this? How could this all be happening?

· 12 ·

Who Gives This Woman?

$\mathcal{A}$bby walked into the kitchen to find her mother sitting at the table in her bathrobe, staring into space. She was surrounded by blank place cards and calligraphy pens. There was a guest list lying in front of her. The scene was more than a little disturbing. It was four in the afternoon on a Monday, and her mother was still in her pj's? Her mother was always up and dressed by eight-thirty! This was all wrong.

It wasn't until Abby was standing right in front of her that her mother noticed she was there. Abby's mother sat up straight, tucked her hair behind her ears and picked up a pen.

"Hey, honey," she said with a wan smile.

"Mom, how long have you been sitting here?" Abby asked, sliding into the chair across from her mother's. There was only one complete place card and the name was written on a severe diagonal.

"Oh, I don't know," her mother replied. "Not long."

Abby's mother picked up a mug, raised it halfway to her lips and then put it down without taking a sip. Abby looked inside. It was full of coffee that had probably been there all day. There was a slight film over the top of the liquid.

"Do you need help?" Abby asked. "I haven't used my calligraphy skills in a while, but it's probably like riding a bike."

Her mother put her pen down and sighed. "Actually, that would be great. My wrist is still bothering me a bit. . . . I guess I haven't gotten that much done today."

"Mom . . . are you okay?"

"Just a little tired." Her mother flashed that almost smile again. "It's been a long couple of nights."

Abby felt as if her heart were in her throat, blocking the air. "Have you . . . talked to Dad at all?" Her father had slept on the pullout couch in his office the night before.

"Not really. Not at all, actually. We've gotten very good at avoiding each other," her mother said. "Abby,

194

I don't want you to worry. This is just a—a rough patch. Everything's going to be fine, I'm sure."

But she didn't sound too convinced.

"Are Carol and Tucker around?" Abby asked.

"They've been out all day. I think they were meeting with the travel agent about the honeymoon and then running some errands," her mother said. "At least they're going ahead with it. I'd hate for your father and me to be ruining this for your sister."

But you already are, Abby thought, remembering how pale her sister had looked at the dress shop, and again at the shower. Part of her wanted to say something, but she knew the last thing her mother needed was more pressure. There was so much to keep to herself these days: Italy, Noah, Tucker, her feelings about her mom and dad. She was starting to wonder if she should bother talking at all.

"Mom, why don't you go take a bath or something?" Abby suggested. "I can work on these for a while."

"You sure?" her mother asked, brightening a bit at the suggestion.

"Definitely. It might even be fun," Abby lied.

"Okay. Thanks, Abby." Her mother got up and kissed the top of her head. "What would I do without you?"

Abby was overcome by guilt. What if things didn't work out between her parents? Carol would be living in Colorado, Abby would be in Italy and her mom would be here all alone.

Or would she? Would her parents still run the Dove's Roost together, or would they have to dissolve the business? Would they all have to move?

It was just too much to handle. She wished she could have discussed some of it with her mother. But with her mother looking so tired and out of it, now didn't seem like the time for a mother–daughter heart-to-heart. It seemed like the time for a nice, long nap.

* * *

"I can't believe you haven't heard from Student XChange yet," Delila said as she tore into her supersize fries. "What are they trying to do, give you an ulcer?"

"Actually, I did hear," Abby said dully. She wasn't even sure if she wanted to tell her yet, but she needed someone to get happy about something. She glanced up from her untouched salad to witness Delila's reaction.

"Omigod! They rejected you? What's *wrong* with them?"

"Nothing," Abby said. "I got in."

"You did?" Delila screeched. She leaned forward, her eyes huge. "When were you going to tell me about this? When did you get the letter? What did your parents say? Why is my voice all squeaky?"

Abby snorted a laugh. "I'm not totally sure I'm going to go."

"You're kidding. You *have* to go." Delila's face dropped. "Oh, God. This isn't because of Noah, is it? I mean, he's hot, but you guys just started dating."

"It's not Noah," Abby said. "The thought of leaving him *does* give me instant acid reflux. Still, it's not him."

"Then it has to be Dave and Phoebe. Do you need me to talk to them?"

"I haven't even asked them yet," Abby said quietly.

"What? Ab! Why are you sabotaging this?"

"I don't know, Delila. I mean, you saw my parents the other day. I don't think now is the best time to tell them I'm bailing on them for a year."

"Abby, I know you're upset about your parents, but you're not responsible for their relationship," Delila said. "You can't let a couple of little fights get in the way of an experience like this."

"My dad moved into his office, remember?" Abby said morosely. "My parents have stopped speaking entirely. It's not a couple of little fights."

Delila took a deep breath and shoveled a few fries into her mouth. "It's your decision. I just think you'd have to be crazy nuts to pass this up."

"I'm not passing it up . . . yet," Abby said, lifting her shoulders. "I've just got other things to concentrate on right now."

Like how to put my family back together in time for Carol's wedding.

Across the food court she saw Christopher walk in with a bunch of his friends.

Abby caught his eye. She waved and he raised his eyebrows. He said something to his buddies, then sauntered over.

"Check it out," he said, hurling something at her from a few feet away.

Abby snatched it out of the air before it could land in her salad.

"Nice reflexes," Delila said, rolling her eyes.

"It's your press pass," Christopher said with a grin. Abby gathered the cord up in her hand. Sure enough, the laminated card was decorated in red, white and blue and had the Revolution logo at the top. Her own name was printed right over the words *All Access*.

"My dad just gave them to me," Christopher said. "You psyched?"

"Definitely," Abby said, mustering a smile.

"We'll pick you up Wednesday at five."

"Sounds like a plan," Abby replied.

"Later."

Christopher moved off to join his friends on the line at Nathan's hot dogs. Delila sat up straight.

"Don't say hello to me!" she called out. "I don't exist!"

"Whatever, freak," Christopher said over his shoulder.

Abby shoved the pass into her bag. It was amazing how something that had seemed like so much fun last week now felt like it was going to just be one more chore.

"What's that all about?" Delila asked, looking down at her fries.

"We're going to the Revolution game next Wednesday. His dad got us press passes."

"Oh. Uh-huh," Delila said. She studied the interior of her fry box.

"What does that mean?" Abby asked.

"Nothing," Delila said. "Just wondering what Noah thinks about this little date."

"It's not a date. You know it's not a date," Abby said. "And Noah doesn't think anything about it because I haven't told him."

Delila shook her head slowly. "If it's not a date then why haven't you told Noah about it?"

"It's . . . complicated," Abby replied, squirming.

"I'm sure it is," Delila said. She raised her eyebrows and then turned her head away.

"What? What's your problem?" Abby asked, her face feeling hot.

"Nothing! I just think you need to make some decisions about your life," Delila said. "Are you going to Italy or not? Do you want an honest relationship with Noah or not? Are you going to tell Carol about Tucker or not? In case you haven't noticed, they're getting married in a week and a half and you still haven't made a decision. You're all over the place, Ab."

"Like I don't know this? You're supposed to be my friend, D. Can't you be a little supportive?"

"I am being supportive! I'm telling you—pick a lane!"

"Gee, thanks for the advice," Abby said. "I'll get right on that. It's not that simple, Delila."

"Whatever. I need more fries," Delila said, getting up and grabbing her bag. "I'll meet you by the exit."

What is up her *butt?* Abby wondered as Delila stormed away. Abby was the one who should be freaking out here. Her life was the one in shambles. And Delila was the one person she had always been able to count on.

Was she supposed to handle all of this alone?

. . .

Abby and Becky had been sitting in the craft room for hours. The various clippings, suggestions and orders from Abby's parents were splayed out across the drafting table. No wonder Becky had been such a mess the past two weeks. The whole thing was totally overwhelming.

"Well, I guess that's it then," Becky said, getting ready to go. "It'll either be totally gorgeous or the most hideous fun-house wedding you've ever seen."

"It won't be hideous," Abby assured her.

"I just don't want to screw this up," Becky said, gathering the papers into a pile. "I mean, it's *Carol's* wedding."

"You won't screw it up," Abby said. "You were obviously born to do this, Becky."

"Thanks. That means a lot coming from a Beaumont," Becky said with a smile.

"Yeah. Not so much from this Beaumont."

"You sell yourself short. You did a fabulous job with the shower and you've helped me out with these details more than you know," Becky said. Abby felt her face break into a grin. "So, you coming?" Becky asked.

"Nah. I need to finish the place cards for the Citron wedding." Abby stretched her arms over her head. "A Dove's Roost daughter's job is never done."

"Well, thanks again for going over this with me," Becky said. "I really needed a second opinion."

Just then the door to the craft room opened and Abby's dad stuck his head in. Abby's heart caught, skipping over itself in nervous surprise. Her dad had been practically invisible all week—going for long walks in the morning, turning in early and taking meetings outside the Roost. She had barely seen him since he'd walked out on Carol's shower and he looked terrible. His eyes were tired, his chin was stubbly and even though it had only been a few days, somehow he actually seemed thinner.

"A second opinion on what?" he asked lightly.

"Oh—on—my hair," Becky said, laughing easily. "I'm trying to decide whether to go back to curly."

"Well, I always liked your curls," Abby's dad said, crossing over to the drafting table. He patted Abby on the head and smiled. "But then, I've always had a soft spot for curly-haired girls."

"Thanks, Mr. Beaumont. I'll take your vote into account," Becky said, heading for the door. Then she gave Abby a quick wave and closed the door behind her.

"So, Abby, what are you doing in here?" her father asked.

"Finishing the place cards for Saturday." Abby pulled a few cards toward her. "What's up?"

"I was just going to pick up the supplies for the favors."

"I think the box is in the corner," Abby told him. Her heart pounded. She knew this was the perfect time to ask him what was going on.

"Here we go," he said, lifting up the box of favors. He brought it over to the table and leaned it on the edge. "How's your job going?"

"Fine," Abby said. She looked up at her father, who looked so sad. She just couldn't hold it in anymore. "Dad, what is going on with you and Mom?" Abby blurted out.

Her father sighed. "It's complicated, honey."

There was that word again. *Complicated.*

"So, explain it to me." Abby spun her chair so she was facing him. "Because as far as I can tell this whole thing is insane."

"Abby, there are just some things you can't understand until you're older," her father said. "Until you've been in a relationship."

Abby's face burned. Sometimes it was like her dad had forgotten to notice that she had grown up. "I am in a relationship, Dad," she said.

His eyebrows shot up. "You are? With whom?"

"With . . . Noah Spencer," she said.

"Really?" Her father smiled. "I thought he was a poop head."

"Dad! I was in, like, third grade when I said that," Abby said, laughing. "Things change."

Her father's face quickly darkened. "Yes. Unfortunately they do."

"What does that mean?" Abby felt a pit in her stomach. "You haven't—I mean, the way you feel about Mom hasn't changed, has it?"

"No!" her father said quickly. Then he sighed and looked at the floor. "Abby, I really don't think—"

"Okay. I'm sorry. Forget it," she said, turning back toward her work. He thought she was immature? Fine. Let him think what he wanted. But wasn't it he and her mother who were the ones acting like little kids? They were the ones making public scenes, refusing to talk to each other and messing up the whole family. All of this because they couldn't agree on a few wedding details. How grown-up was that?

"Good night, Abby," her father said. He reached out to put his hand on her shoulder.

Abby shrank away from his touch, then tried to ignore the hurt look on his face. Maybe her parents weren't going to let her in on what was going on, but she wasn't going to hide her own feelings anymore. She already had enough to keep inside.

· 13 ·

Impediments

Abby loaded the CD into the burner, waited for it to copy, slapped on the label and then slipped it into the jewel box. She had dozens and dozens and dozens of CDs to make for Carol's wedding. And she was only on number eight. The work was mindless, and as she carried on she couldn't stop her brain from racing on to other things.

This wedding is actually going to happen. How did I let it get this far? Abby pulled another finished CD, warm and fresh from the CD-ROM tray. In three days' time, her sister would be Mrs. Tucker Robb, never having known that Tucker was fooling around behind her back. Maybe.

How can I let this happen?

But the questions were pointless, because she already knew. She'd been hoping for some kind of divine intervention. She'd hoped Carol would figure it out on her own or that someone else would figure it out and tell her. Abby didn't want to be the one to break her sister's heart, so she'd opted for the easy way out—avoidance.

I suck, Abby thought as she looked down at the CD label. Carol and Tucker's names were intertwined in an elaborate script against a blue backdrop. *I totally suck as a sister.*

Just then the front door slammed. Startled, Abby pushed herself up off the floor and looked out the window. There was Tucker stomping across the front yard toward his truck. Clearly he was all riled up about something.

Suddenly a thought popped into Abby's head. *Maybe this is it.* The something big she'd been waiting for. Maybe Carol had found out what Tucker was up to and had finally broken it off.

Please, Abby thought. *Please, please, please . . . What?* What did she want? For Tucker to be innocent and everything to be okay or for Carol to have found out Tucker was a sleaze and broken it off?

She had no idea what to hope for.

Abby rounded the corner at the bottom of the stairs. She paused when she saw Carol's tiny form, huddled at the kitchen table, her face in her hands.

Her back was shaking and she was clearly crying. Abby felt as if her heart were breaking wide open.

"Carol? What's wrong?"

With a loud sniffle, Carol lifted her head. Her face was streaked with tears and her nose was all red. She looked just like she had the first time she saw footage of animals stuck in an oil slick.

"Tucker. He . . . he . . ."

Is a lying, cheating scum sucker? Abby thought.

"He thinks I'm a Bridezilla!" Carol finished. She grabbed a tissue out of the box in the middle of the table and blew her nose noisily. "He says all I've talked about for the last month is the wedding. He says that I've become totally obsessed. But it's not true, right?"

Carol looked at Abby hopefully. The last thing Abby wanted to do was agree with the scum sucker at the moment, but she hesitated. There was some truth to what he was saying.

"It's not true," Carol said again. "Is it?"

"No," Abby said finally. "No, Carol. You're fine."

Carol looked so miserable Abby didn't know what to do. So Abby did what her mom did when Abby was upset—she sat down next to Carol and she rubbed her back. It was always comforting when her mom did it. She hoped she could have the same effect.

"He said I've forgotten what this whole thing is really about—him and me and the rest of our lives." Carol was crumpling and uncrumpling her napkin. "Like I could really forget about that. All *he* ever talks about is Colorado and how much I'll love it and how our bedroom faces the sunset over the mountains. . . ."

"Well, that sounds nice," Abby said.

"Yeah, I know," Carol replied, nodding. "But do you know what else he said?"

"What?"

"He said that if I need an illustration of what wedding-obsessing can do to people, I should just look at my parents," Carol said, her jaw dropping a bit. "I mean, I'm upset enough already that Mom and Dad are practically divorced—did he really have to rub it in?"

"Don't say that," Abby said quickly. The very thought sent a wave of a nausea right through her. "They're not practically divorced."

"I know. I'm sorry," Carol said. "I'm just upset."

"Well . . . see? People say things they don't mean when they're upset. Maybe Tucker didn't mean to say that."

"You think?" Carol asked with a sniffle.

Why am I defending him? Abby wondered. But as she looked into her sister's big wet eyes, she knew. She was defending him because Carol loved him. In that moment, it was that simple.

"Don't worry. I'm sure he'll be coming through that door with a big bouquet of I'm-sorry flowers any minute. Where did he go, anyway?"

"To Andrew's hotel," Carol said. "So, you don't think I'm wedding-obsessed?"

"Nah." Abby pushed her sister's hair behind her

shoulder, reached her arm around her and gave her a little squeeze. "You're fine."

The doorbell rang and Abby got up to answer it. She opened the door to find a guy about her age standing on the doorstep with a large box.

"Delivery for Carol Beaumont," he said.

Abby looked over at her sister, who dried her eyes and got up from the table. She signed the guy's clipboard and took the box.

"Oh!" she said, suddenly sounding bright and cheery. "It's the menus!" Carol lifted the lid of the box and pulled out a white card with a ribbon tied at the top. The wedding menu was printed down the center.

"Oh . . . pretty," Abby said, trying to sound as peppy as her sister. "Wow. You guys didn't go for simple when it came to the food, huh?"

Abby looked at Carol, whose face had suddenly crumpled. "This is all wrong!" she wailed.

"Is there a problem?" the guy asked, paling slightly.

"Yes! Yes there's a problem," Carol said, shoving the box at Abby. She held the menu up with both hands in front of the guy's face. "See this ribbon? What color would you say this ribbon is? Huh? What color?"

"Blue?" the guy asked, glancing desperately at Abby.

"Um, Carol? Let's just—"

"Well *duh,* Mr. Rhodes Scholar, but what *shade* of blue?" Carol practically screeched.

"I—I don't—" the guy stammered.

"Don't you do this for a *living?*" Carol shouted. She walked forward and the guy retreated a couple of steps. "This ribbon is *supposed* to be *violet* blue. I don't know what *this* color is, but it is *not* violet blue!"

"Carol," Abby said cautiously. "Calm down–"

"Don't 'calm down' me, Abby. My invitations had a violet blue ribbon!" Carol's eyes grew wide. Her hand was flailing around wildly and the delivery guy kept a close eye on it like it was some kind of weapon. "They're supposed to match! Is that too much to ask? I mean, I didn't want much, but I figured I could at least have that!"

Carol dissolved into sobs again, holding the menu over her face.

"I–I'm sorry," the guy said, swallowing nervously. "Of course we'll reprint them for you at no extra charge."

"Oh yeah? When?" Carol demanded, throwing her arms down again. "The wedding is this weekend! How are you going to do it before *Saturday?*"

The poor delivery guy stumbled back a few more steps and Abby realized it was about time to defuse the situation. She stepped in front of her sister.

"Carol, you need to chill," she said.

"But this is my *wedding!*" Carol blubbered.

"Yes, Carol," Abby said, forcing herself to sound calm. "The fact that this is your wedding is not something that I haven't noticed. Trust me." Then Abby turned to the delivery guy and gave him a sympathetic smile. "These are fine, thank you." The delivery guy just nodded, then promptly turned and ran. Abby pulled Carol back inside and closed the door before she could say anything else. She walked by her and dropped the box on the kitchen table. "Okay, Carol. Deep breaths. Come on. It's gonna be okay."

Carol sucked wind, bracing her hands against the counter. "I'm okay . . . I'm . . . I'm okay," she said.

Abby took a deep breath and pushed her hair back from her face. "What the heck *was* that?" she asked.

"I know! You'd think they could get one little thing like a ribbon color right!" Carol exclaimed, grabbing a tissue and dabbing at her eyes.

"Not that!" Abby cried. "That!" She pointed toward the window, behind which the sound of squealing tires could now be heard. "You scared the crap out of him because of a ribbon, which, by the way, looks *exactly* the same as your invitations!"

Carol looked down at the tearstained menu in her hands as if she'd never seen it before. "It's . . . it's not. It's a different shade of . . ."

Her hand reached out shakily and she grasped the top of the chair at the head of the table. The menu card fluttered to the tabletop and Carol closed her eyes.

"Oh my God. Tucker's right," she said. "I am a Bridezilla."

"It's okay," Abby said after a long pause. "The first step is acceptance."

Carol's eyes popped open. "This isn't funny, Abby," she said. "I'm exactly what we always despised. I'm exactly what we always promised we'd never be."

"Carol . . ."

"I need to get out of here," Carol said, grabbing her purse from the kitchen counter. "I need to be alone for a while."

Before Abby could say anything else, her sister was out the door.

Menu

Cold Vodka and Honeydew Melon Soup

*Garden Salad with Pine Nuts
and Raspberry Vinaigrette*

*Tricolor Farfalle with Capers, Black Olives,
Olive Oil, Garlic and Fresh Basil*

*Roast Rack of Lamb with
Rosemary Mashed Potatoes
Or
Red Snapper Provençale
with Fresh Vegetables*

*Wedding Cake
Viennese Display
Rice Pudding
Chocolate-Covered Strawberries*

"Thanks for doing this with me," Abby said as Noah turned his car into the dry cleaner's parking lot.

"When Carol bailed with the van I had no idea what to do."

"Well, you called the right guy," Noah said. He yanked up the parking brake. "Just call me Wedding Man."

"Okay, that may be the dorkiest thing you've ever said." Abby laughed.

"Yeah. That was pretty bad," Noah said.

They got out of the car together and headed inside. Carol and Abby had planned a whole afternoon of errand running. When Carol had disappeared, Abby had realized it was time to flip into true maid of honor mode. It was her responsibility to pull off this wedding no matter *how* she felt about it.

Inside, Abby handed the pink claim ticket to the man behind the counter. He disappeared into the back. Abby turned around to find her father walking through the door.

"Dad!" she said, surprised.

"Abby!" he replied.

"Hey, Mr. Beaumont," Noah said.

"Oh, hello." He seemed confused to find them there. Abby's father handed his ticket to the counter person and then turned to Abby. "How's your mother doing?" he asked.

"You still haven't talked to her?"

"Not yet. Things are–"

"Complicated. I know," Abby said. Her father's eyes looked so sad she could barely stand it. "Actually, Dad, she's a mess. Kind of like you."

"I'm not a mess," her father said, pulling out his wallet.

A ton of change, lint and crumpled pieces of paper came with it and scattered all over the floor. Noah dropped down to pick them up and Abby's father flushed. He rubbed his hand over his face—hard—as if he were trying to keep himself awake.

"All I was trying to do was give Phoebe a wedding she would always remember," he said. "That's all I wanted."

Noah stood up, his hands full, and exchanged a glance with Abby.

"You mean Carol," Abby said, her heart racing.

"What?" her father asked.

"You mean you wanted to give Carol a wedding to remember," Abby said. "You said Phoebe."

Her father's brow furrowed. "I did?"

The guy who had taken her father's ticket came back and hung his tux on the rod between the registers. Noah handed her dad his things.

"Thanks, Noah," her father said. He counted out the money he owed the cleaner. Abby watched him as her mind slowly put everything into place.

A candy store wedding was totally her father's kitschy style. And at the stationery store he'd told them that if *he* were getting married, he would use those modern invitations from the red book. Red was, in fact, *his* favorite color, and he tried to push nouvelle cuisine on every VIC that walked through the Dove's Roost door.

Her dad hadn't been planning Carol's dream wedding. He'd been planning the wedding of *his* dreams. The one he wished he could have had for himself and his wife. For Phoebe.

• • •

"Where do you want this?" Noah asked, holding up a box full of light blue votive candles.

"I think my mom's showing a VIC around the Roost so let's just bring it to my room for now," Abby said.

As they trudged up the stairs, all Abby could think about was crashing on her bed and taking a nap. This had been one long, emotionally draining, wedding-intensive day. Her brain couldn't stop going over her revelation about her dad. Her back hurt from all the lifting and lugging and packing and unpacking. Wasn't back pain something only old people complained about?

The second Abby dropped the dry-cleaning bag full of linens on her bed, the doorbell rang. She sighed heavily, casting a longing look at her pillows.

"That's probably another delivery. I'll be right back."

She trotted down the stairs, through the kitchen, and opened the door.

"Hey! Ready to go?" Christopher asked brightly.

"Go? Where?" she asked. She looked down at his Revolution T-shirt and slapped her hand over her mouth. "Oh, God! The game!"

Christopher's face fell. "You forgot?"

"It's been really crazy around here lately. I'm sorry," Abby said, stepping back. "Come in for a second. I just . . . I need to get changed."

What she really needed was a shower and a long sleep, but that was clearly not going to happen. Christopher followed her back upstairs, chatting excitedly.

"So we'll definitely get to check out the locker room. And we'll take pictures with the players, which will be awesome and—" Abby opened the door to her bedroom and the chatter instantly stopped.

Noah was standing in the middle of the room holding a piece of paper. He looked stunned and confused. Then he glanced up, saw Christopher and clenched his jaw.

"Are you . . . going to Italy?" Noah asked, holding out the page.

Abby's throat instantly went dry.

Oh.

Crap.

"How did you . . . ?"

"I was looking for a pen," Noah said, glancing quickly at Christopher. "Were you even going to tell me about this?"

"Wait a minute, you got in?" Christopher said. He stepped around Abby so he could face her, his grin huge. "You're coming?"

"Hold on. *He's* going?" Noah's voice shifted from shock to anger. "You have to be kidding me."

"Okay, wait. Everyone just hold on a second," Abby said. "Noah. I was going to tell you—"

"We are going to have so much fun, yo," Christopher said.

"Christopher, you are not helping," Abby said.

"You know what, forget it," Noah said. "You two go to Italy and I'll just go home."

He walked past them and ran down the stairs at record speed. Abby shot Christopher a look, then took off after Noah.

"Noah!"

"What is *he* doing here?" Noah asked. His hand was on the doorknob. Christopher stopped in his tracks and hovered behind Abby.

"We're going to a Revolution game," Christopher said.

"Oh. Really? So that's why you couldn't come over for dinner tonight, Abby? Because you were going out with *him*? This just gets better and better!"

Abby brought her hand to her forehead. "I'm sorry. I–"

"For what? For lying or for dating another guy?" Noah asked.

"He *is* just my friend," Abby said. "And you're more than that. You know that."

"Then why lie to me?" Noah asked. There was so much pain in his eyes that it hurt Abby to look into them. "Why are you keeping all this major stuff from me and going out with other guys behind my back?"

"It's not like that," Abby said simply. She was so exhausted, she didn't even have it in her to argue.

"Well, it sure looks that way to me," Noah said.

Then he turned and stormed out, slamming the

door behind him. Abby's eyes filled with tears and she took a deep breath.

"Anything I can do?" Christopher asked.

"You're gonna have to go without me," she said.

"Ab, come on. I know you're upset, but we're talking about all-access passes here!" he said.

"I know! It's just . . . there's too much going on around here for me to go out and have fun," Abby said, barely holding it together. "I'm sorry, Christopher. Tell your dad I said thanks."

"Okay," Christopher said with a sigh. "Well, call me if you need anything. And for the record, I'm psyched about Italy and I'm sorry about Cakeboy."

"Yeah," Abby said, her eyes welling up with tears. "Me too."

Abby walked Christopher to the door. As soon as he was gone, Abby started upstairs to commence her nervous breakdown. She could barely catch her breath. First Tucker, then Carol, then her dad, then Noah. Everything was falling apart.

Suddenly a cell phone rang, stopping her in her tracks. It wasn't hers. It wasn't her mom's wedding march, or Carol's phone, which played some classical tune. Abby saw a silver cell on the counter. Tucker's phone.

Don't do it, a little voice in her mind warned. *You really shouldn't.*

Abby grabbed the phone and hit the talk button. "Hello?"

"Oh . . . sorry," a girl's voice said. "I must have the wrong number."

"Wait! Are you looking for Tucker?" Abby asked. Her heart was pounding so hard, she was amazed she was even able to speak.

"Yes. . . ."

"I can give him a message," Abby said, biting her lip. "I'm his sister."

She gripped the countertop. What was she doing? Had the events of the last twenty-four hours sent her completely over the edge?

"Oh, great!" the girl said. "This is Margery. He's a little late and I just wanted to make sure he's still coming. Is he already on his way to the restaurant?"

Margery? I thought her name was Melissa! Is he having two affairs?

"I don't know," Abby improvised. "He . . . just left. Where did he say he was going again . . . ?" she said as if she were trying to remember.

"The Seascape, right? I hope he didn't forget," Margery said.

I should totally be a detective, Abby thought.

"Yes! That's it! The Seascape!" she said. "I'm sure he'll be there any minute. Bye!"

Abby pressed her thumb into the off button—hard. The rat. How could he do this to her sister? How could he be seeing not one, but two women?

And how was she ever going to prove it?

And suddenly Abby knew what she had to do. She ran upstairs, grabbed her keys and the digital camera she'd gotten for her birthday and headed outside. She was on a mission. At least it gave her something to do other than sit in her room and obsess about Noah.

As soon as she stepped out the door, she realized the flaw in her plan—Carol had the van. The sun was just starting to go down and Abby's mom was still inside with her VIC. Abby looked down at her key to her mom's Avalon. She was only supposed to use it in emergencies. This definitely qualified.

Abby jogged over to the car, got in and pulled out to the road. She turned right and headed for the water.

Fifteen minutes later, she eased over to the side of the road, right across from the Seascape. It was the newest restaurant in Watertown and sat overlooking the docks at the edge of town. The front windows were big and bright, and Abby could see the couples dining inside at candlelit tables. It looked like a very romantic setting, most of the tables just big enough to accommodate two.

Suddenly Abby saw him. Tucker. Walking along the sidewalk toward the restaurant, carrying a bottle of wine. All of Abby's emotions seemed to come to a head at that moment—her heartbreak over Noah, her confusion and anger over her parents, her resentment of Tucker, her annoyance at Delila for exploding at the mall, her irritation at Carol for getting married and leaving her. All she wanted to do was get out of the car, walk over to the restaurant and punch that Tucker in his stupid cheating head.

Get a grip, she told herself. *You're not going to drop anyone, least of all the Colorado cowboy.*

Abby slouched down in her seat, peeking through the window. Tucker walked into the restaurant. A pretty girl with blond hair got up from her table when she saw him and smiled. Tucker stepped over and greeted her with a kiss. It wasn't entirely on the lips, but it wasn't entirely on the cheek either. He definitely caught half and half. Not the kiss of a mere friend.

Abby's fingers instinctively curled into fists. That was when she felt the camera in her hand. In her shock she had completely forgotten about it. But looking at it now . . . it seemed so petty. She didn't want her sister to see this. She didn't want photographic proof of Tucker's infidelity burned into Carol's mind forever.

She was just going to have to tell Carol what she'd seen, and hope that her sister believed her.

· 14 ·

The Big Day

$\mathcal{A}$bby lay on her bed wondering if life could possibly get any worse. It was later that night and she desperately needed to talk to someone, but so far had had no luck. Delila's cell phone went directly to voice mail and she wasn't home when Abby had tried her house. Abby had left Noah three messages and gotten no reply. Christopher had left *her* a message, but she didn't want to call him back and hear about all the fun she'd missed. Her mother had gone out for a last-minute fitting for her mother-of-the-bride dress, leaving Abby and her dad to eat dinner alone. Abby had considered saying something to her father, but he looked haggard enough already eating his sad lonely bowl of soup. She just didn't have it in her to make him feel any worse. Her sister still wasn't back. And neither was Tucker, which probably meant he was out there right now, making out with Margery in the back of some car.

This had to be what they called rock bottom. Only Abby felt she was about ten layers of igneous crap *beneath* rock bottom. She sighed and turned her head to look at her clock. It was one a.m. Sleep was apparently not going to happen.

Suddenly she heard the sound of a car pulling into the driveway. She got up and rushed to the window. It was Carol! Thank goodness. Abby had to tell her about tonight and she had to tell her now.

Except that right behind the van was Tucker's truck.

What the . . .

Abby watched as Tucker and Carol both got out of their cars. They walked over to each other and quickly embraced. Then they joined hands and disappeared around the side of the house. They looked positively giddy. Abby sat down on her bed. Why were they so happy? And how was she going to tell Carol that the guy she was clutching fingers with had been out on a date only a few hours ago?

A few minutes later Abby heard the stairs creak. Tucker and Carol went into her room. There was a lot of whispering, shushing and giggling. A few minutes later, the door to Carol's bedroom opened and closed again and there were more footsteps on the stairs.

Abby started for the hall, then heard the front door open and close. She ran back over to the window and what she saw down below in the moonlight made her heart drop.

Carol and Tucker were getting into the truck. With suitcases.

Oh no! Abby thought. She ran downstairs in her nightshirt and socks. *Nonononononono!* Where were they going?

Abby didn't even have time to think of all the reasons to stop them. All she knew was that she *had* to stop them.

She sprinted through the kitchen, out the door and onto the driveway. The truck was already pulling away.

"Carol!" Abby shouted at the top of her lungs. The brake lights lit up at the end of the drive.

"Carol, stop!" Abby cried, running toward them in her bare feet. She was just twenty yards away— could practically feel the steel of the flatbed on her fingertips. The truck turned and disappeared behind the hedge, rumbling off to anywhere.

• • •

"Come on . . . pick up!" Abby was pacing in her bedroom. "Pick up, pick up, pick *up!*"

Carol's voice mail clicked on and Abby slammed the phone down. She had tried both Carol and Tucker's cell phones hundreds of times since they'd left, but neither of them was answering. There was no telling where they were, what they were doing or if they were ever coming back.

They could be eloping, Abby thought for the twenti-eth time that day. It all fit—the sneaking off at night, the giggling, the suitcases. All that coupled with the fact that Carol had realized her Bridezilla status just yesterday afternoon made an elopement seem like a sure bet. But there was just no way Carol would do that to her parents. Especially not without telling them. Abby just couldn't imagine it. After everything her mom and dad had gone through for this wedding, Abby knew that Carol would never take her wedding away from them.

So where the heck was she?

"Okay, think. Where would they have gone?" Abby asked herself. She had already looked through all the papers on Carol's desk, but she decided to try again. Sooner or later her parents, who were putting the finishing touches on their dueling weddings down-stairs, were going to realize the bride was missing. And when they did they were going to come to Abby for an explanation. Ransacking Carol's room seemed like Abby's only option.

Abby let herself into Carol's bedroom and glanced around. If there were no clues on the desk, where Carol seemed to plan her whole life, where else would they be? A bunch of bridal magazines were stacked neatly on Carol's bedside table. At a loss for anything else to do, Abby lifted the first magazine and quickly flipped through it. Nothing. She dropped it on the bed and tried the second. Nothing. She groaned and lifted the third. A pamphlet slipped out from underneath it and fell open on the floor. Abby picked it up and her blood ran cold. No. This was not possible.

The colorful ad was splashed with the headline *Say I Do! Vegas-Style!* Pictured was a happy couple, and walking down the aisle on either side was a snarling Elvis impersonator. On the side flap was a list of wedding packages, and the one at the very top was circled and starred in red ink: the Little White Wedding.

"Oh . . . my . . . God," Abby said breathlessly. "They're eloping!"

• • •

"Noah! Thank you for picking up!" Abby cried, clutching the phone to her ear. "I need your help. I have no idea what to do."

"Are you all right?" Noah asked.

"Yes . . . no . . . I don't know," Abby said.

Just tell him, Abby's mind shouted as she stared down at the brochure. *Noah always knows what to do. You should have listened to him about Tucker ages ago!*

"Noah, I think Carol and Tucker are eloping," she said. "They snuck out last night with suitcases and I just found this Vegas brochure in her room and . . . my parents are going to die!"

She heard an intake of breath at the other end of the line and held her own.

"Why don't you call Johnny Rockets?" Noah said flatly. "I'm sure he'll know exactly what to do."

Abby was so stung she momentarily lost the power to speak.

Staring at the Elvis impersonator on the front of the brochure, Abby realized that she didn't have time to deal with Noah. She didn't have time to think about herself right now. At that very moment her sister could be walking down the aisle, arm linked to a fat man with fake 'burns, about to marry a guy who was cheating on her. She had to do something—now. It was time to cut her losses.

"You know what, Noah? Call me when you're off the pacifier."

She hung up. Noah really wasn't turning out to be the person she thought he was. Apparently she was on her own.

Feeling sick to her stomach, Abby trudged downstairs. She wasn't even sure of where she was going or why. All she could think about was the fact that she had let her sister down. She had put off doing anything constructive about the Tucker situation, and now her sister was off in Sin City, pledging to be his forever. She *was* the worst maid of honor ever.

The kitchen was deserted so Abby wandered into the Roost toward her mother's office. She paused when she saw Becky behind the desk chatting on the phone.

"All right, honey. We'll see you on Saturday, then," Becky said. "Okay, Carol."

"That's Carol?" Abby exploded, racing into the room.

"Okay! Bye!" Becky said, oblivious, then clicked off.

"Becky! I need to talk to her! Where is she? What's she doing?" Abby cried, her heart pounding.

"Abby, calm down," Becky said. "She just said that she and Tucker needed a couple of days off from the wedding insanity. They'll be back Saturday morning."

"Did she say where they were? Where they're staying?" Abby asked, her mouth dry.

"No," Becky said, confused. "What's the matter?"

"Nothing," Abby said, her shoulders slumping. She knew that if she told Becky the wedding was off she would be looking at the business end of a major meltdown. Becky's reaction would be almost as bad as her parents' was going to be. "I'll see you later, Becky. I'm gonna go do something . . . maid-of-honor-ly."

"Oh, Abby. You're so cute," Becky said. "You've always been so antiwedding, but this one's really gotten to you, hasn't it?"

"You have no idea," Abby said.

•   •   •

Saturday morning arrived and Abby was a ball of frayed nerves. Her eyes were dry and tired from an entire night spent online, looking up Vegas wedding chapels. She'd called every last one, searching for some record of Carol and Tucker. Unfortunately she'd come up with nothing. She wandered downstairs, knowing that she had to tell her parents something, but she was afraid to even open her mouth.

Abby's mother was seated at the kitchen table in her silk robe, her hair pulled back in a tasteful chignon, her makeup perfectly applied. She sipped a cup of coffee as she stared into space. Already things didn't look good. The woman may have been coiffed, but on the morning of a wedding she was usually running about frantically, making sure everything was in place. Here it was, the day of her own daughter's wedding—supposedly—and she was catatonic.

"Hey, Mom," Abby said, pouring herself a cup of coffee. "Have you heard from Carol?"

"No, sweetie," her mother said, blinking a few times. "But she said she'd be back in plenty of time." She checked her watch and frowned. "The photographer will be here at one. As long as she's home by twelve. . . ."

Abby heard her father's muffled voice coming from outside as he directed some delivery people toward the backyard. Both she and her mother looked at the wall in the direction his voice was coming from, then returned to their coffee.

"Have you talked to him?" Abby asked, her stomach churning.

"Not today," her mother said. Then she sighed. "Oh, Abby, this whole thing is so stupid."

Yes! Finally! Abby thought, hope searing through her.

"You mean you and Dad?" she asked.

"Yes! Fighting over Carol's wedding?" her mother said, shaking her head. She placed her chin in her hand and gazed at Abby sadly. "How did we get here?"

"Have you asked him that?"

Her mother shrugged. "No. I just . . . I don't know where to start. We've both said some ugly things over the past few weeks, Abby, things I'm sure neither one of us is proud of."

Abby stood up, filled with a new sense of purpose.

Maybe if she could get her parents talking—get them to work things out—she could then sit them down to-gether and tell them what Carol had done. Then they could all figure it out together.

"Where're you going?" her mother asked.

"I've gotta check on something," Abby said. "I'll be right back."

Abby headed outside and around the house to the backyard, where Liam and his flower crew were hard at work. There was no trace of her father. Abby hoped he hadn't already gotten away.

"Hey, Liam!" she called out. "Where's my dad?"

"He went back to his office!" Liam called back.

"Thanks!" Abby replied.

She walked into the ballroom by the back door and stopped dead in the center of the room. "Whoooaaaa . . . ," she said, turning slowly in place as she looked around.

"It's good, right? Not hideous?" Becky asked, clutching her clipboard to her chest.

"Becky, it's . . . wow," Abby said.

The room had never looked so beautiful. Classic white china plates gleamed next to wine and cham-pagne glasses in every color of the rainbow. The all-white rose centerpieces were placed atop candy-striped ribbon bows that trailed out from the middle of the tables and down to the floor. Cascading flower arrangements lined the walls, while more colorful ribbons draped from every corner of the ceiling to the center, transforming the air above into strips of licorice and peppermint. Along one wall was an old-fashioned candy display where guests could put together their own bags of candy favors. The ballroom looked like Wonka's candy factory . . . except it was perfectly elegant.

"I went with all-white flowers and china like we discussed and added the colorful accents," Becky explained, looking around. "If we'd had the centerpieces your dad wanted–"

"It would've been too much," Abby finished.

"Exactly, but if we hadn't added the color, it would've looked like a hospital," Becky said. "So . . . you think I did good?"

"Becky, I think you did great," Abby said sincerely.

"So neither one of them is going to fire me?" Becky asked.

"No one's gonna fire you," Abby said, smiling at Becky. "There may be no wedding, but they're not gonna fire you."

Becky's grin went from huge to nonexistent in record time.

"No wedding? What are you talking about?"

"Wow! This place looks incredible!"

Abby turned around to find Carol standing in the back doorway of the ballroom. She was slightly tan and wore a pair of low-rise jeans and a tank top. She looked glowingly happy.

"You're here!" Abby shouted, running into her sister's arms. "Are you married? Tell me you're not married!"

"What? I'm not married!"

"Oh thank God," Becky said, gripping a chair for support. "But you're getting married, right?"

Carol pressed her teeth together and grimaced. "Well . . ."

"What?" Abby half screamed. "You're not getting married?"

"Um . . . Becky? Could you excuse us for a sec?" Carol asked.

"Sure," Becky said, her hand to her forehead. "I think I need to go faint anyway."

Becky walked off and Carol led Abby over to one of the cushioned chairs. Abby sat down and turned toward her sister.

"Carol, listen, I have to talk to you. I don't really know how to tell you this but—" Abby took a deep breath and pressed her lips together. "Tucker is cheating on you."

At that moment Tucker stepped through the back door, tan and grinning. Both his and Carol's faces dropped. "What?" they said in unison.

Then Carol cracked up laughing. This was not the reaction she had anticipated.

"He's not having an affair," Carol said, looking at Tucker, who walked over to stand by her side.

"Yes he is!" Abby replied. "I saw him! He met up with some girl named Margery the other night at the Seascape and he brought her wine! And they kissed! And not only that, but he's been having secret conversations with another one named Melissa . . . begging her not to give up on him and all this stuff!"

As Abby continued to babble, Carol gradually

stopped smiling. She eyed Tucker warily, as if she weren't quite sure she knew him. Meanwhile, Abby didn't hear him denying anything. He just stood there, taking it all in, while clenching and unclenching his jaw.

"Go ahead, tell her!" Abby said, feeling triumphant. "You know I'm right."

Tucker's eyes were full of hurt, which just made Abby want to heave. What was she supposed to do? Feel guilty that she'd called him out on betraying her sister?

"Tucker?" Carol said.

"Look . . . they're just . . . friends," Tucker said, turning to Carol.

"You don't have any friends named Melissa and Margery," Carol said.

"Yeah, I do . . . now," Tucker said, clearly searching for words.

"Now? Now when? Since when?" Carol asked.

"It's not what you think," Tucker said. He broke off and looked at the floor, his hands on his hips. Then he slowly shook his head and sighed. "All right, forget it. I'm bad at lying."

He looked down at Carol, who looked petrified. "Melissa teaches a vegetarian cooking class and she owns the Seascape. It's all vegetarian and it's really good. You'd love it," he said.

Carol tilted her head and stared at him. Tucker cleared his throat.

"Anyway, I've been taking Melissa's class, you know, as a wedding present for you," he said. "So I could cook for you once we were married."

Abby's mouth dropped open. Carol placed her hand over her heart and stood up, looking like she was about to cry. "Really?" she said.

"Yeah," Tucker said. "Margery's in my class and we went to the Seascape to sort of support Melissa. A bunch of people from class were there, actually. All over the restaurant." He turned to Abby at this point. "And if you overheard me pleading with Melissa it was probably because I was asking for private classes. I kept . . . screwing up the spinach quiche," he said sheepishly, scratching at the back of his head. "It kept coming out like spinach *soup*."

Oh, God. If this is true, then I'm an idiot, Abby thought. *I'm the biggest idiot in Idiotville.*

"Wait! I even have her card!" Tucker announced. He pulled out his wallet and sifted though it, finally producing a business card. Carol looked down at it, her eyes gleaming. "I wanted it to be a surprise, so . . . surprise."

"Tucker! This is the sweetest . . ." Carol reached up and threw her arms around Tucker, who hugged her back tightly.

"But . . . you brought . . . wine," Abby said feebly. "You kissed her."

"The Seascape doesn't have a liquor license, so it's bring your own," Tucker said. "And yeah, that whole kiss thing was totally embarrassing. I went for her cheek and missed. It was mortifying. Especially considering her husband was just coming back from the bathroom."

"Oh."

Abby wished more than anything that she could turn time back to that night on the wharf when she and Tucker had started to get to know each other. If she could go back to that moment and take a completely different trajectory, she would. Because now, standing there with him, she realized she had never bothered to know him at all. She had overheard a couple of conversations and made up an entire persona for him that didn't exist. He wasn't the fake, scheming, cheating jerk she had conjured. He was the man she had thought he was that night—a sincere, funny, kind, thoughtful guy who clearly loved her sister. All this time she'd been suspicious of him and all this time he'd just been working on a gift for Carol. A very cool, thoughtful gift. If only she'd just talked to him after that first phone call like Noah had suggested. It would have made the last few weeks a lot easier.

"Tucker, I'm so sorry," Abby said. She felt sick. "I feel awful. I just—"

"You were just looking out for Carol. I get it," Tucker said. "But I hope you trust me now."

"Yeah. Of course," Abby said. Her mind was still reeling, but she was able to realize that it was time to let go. Time to back off and let her sister be happy. She was even relieved.

"Okay, um . . . not to abruptly change the subject, but I'm confused. Did you or did you not go to Vegas?" Abby asked.

"We almost went to Vegas," Carol said, lacing her

fingers through Tucker's. "But by the time we got to the airport we'd changed our minds and ended up in Cancún."

"Cancún! But I found this brochure for quickie weddings!"

"Yeah, we thought about eloping," Carol explained. "But in the end we realized it didn't make sense. That none of this makes sense, actually," she said, looking around at the decorations. "I've been dreaming about that internship my entire college career. I don't want to give that up."

"And I don't want her to," Tucker put in. "I didn't want her to end up resenting me years from now. I mean, you hear all these stories about people giving up on their dreams and then realizing it so much later. . . ."

"Hello! Haven't I been saying this all along?" Abby asked.

"You really never miss an 'I told you so,' do you?" Carol replied.

"Never," Abby said. "But didn't you turn down the internship?"

"I called them from Cancún and they said they had been hoping I'd change my mind," Carol said. "They hadn't offered the job to anyone else yet."

"Wow. They must really want you," Abby said.

"She is just that good," Tucker put in, kissing Carol on the cheek. For the first time witnessing their intimacy didn't make Abby physically ill. Tucker wasn't kissing anyone else on the side! Whoo-hoo!

"So . . . what are you two going to do?" Abby said, glancing at their clutched hands. "You obviously didn't break up."

"Oh, no," Tucker said. "We're still engaged. It's just gonna be a long engagement. We're going to get married after we've had some time to figure some more stuff out. Like where we both want to live and what we both want to do. We're not in the right places in our lives yet, but we will be."

"Look! We even got these tattoos on our ring fingers as a sign of our commitment," Carol said.

Carol held up her hand and Abby pulled it toward her. Written in brown ink around her sister's ring finger was the name Tucker in script. Abby grabbed Tucker's hand and saw her sister's name etched onto his skin as well.

"Wow. Cool," Abby said. Carol and Tucker shared a quick kiss.

Abby looked at her sister—at the peaceful, happy glow on her face—and sighed. This was what her sister really wanted.

"I'm happy for you guys," Abby said.

"Good," Carol replied. "I'm happy for us, too."

"Well, I'm gonna go call my family at the hotel and tell them what's going on," Tucker said, knocking his fists together. "Wish me luck."

"Good luck!" Abby and Carol said in unison. With another quick kiss Tucker was gone, leaving Abby and Carol in the middle of the ballroom.

"Okay," Abby said, slapping her palms down on

her thighs. "So what do we do about the fact that Mom and Dad are going to murder you?"

Carol bit her lip. "They are, aren't they? They're totally going to lose it."

"Uh . . . yeah," Abby said.

"And look what an awesome job they did," Carol said. "It's exactly like what they both wanted."

Abby looked up and felt something stir inside her chest. She trailed her gaze over the streaming ribbons, the white roses, the gemstone glasses and the strewn white petals. Carol couldn't have been more right. This was exactly the wedding her parents had always wanted. The English garden wedding her mother had never had for herself. The mod candy store wedding her father had never had for himself. All rolled into one. Becky had pulled off both her parents' dream weddings at once. And it was gorgeous.

"Well, I guess I'll go get this over with," Carol said.

"Wait!" Abby said, standing. She grabbed her sister's wrist, her heart pounding. "I have a better idea."

· 15 ·

Cold Feet

"Okay, we don't have much time," Abby said as she, Tucker and Carol ran for the van. "We gotta get you guys back here and dressed before the photographer comes."

"I still can't believe you're going to Italy," Carol said. She shook her head back and forth in disbelief, like she'd been doing for the last fifteen minutes. "I can't believe you haven't even told Mom and Dad."

"Carol, can we focus here?" Abby said. "Wedding first, Italy later."

"Maybe we should split up," Tucker suggested. "I

can go to one place and you guys can go to the other. We'll meet back here in an hour."

Just then, Delila's Mustang pulled into the driveway and rolled to a stop right next to Abby. And sitting right there in the passenger seat was Christopher Marshall. These were two people who had never been alone together in their lives. Abby was totally shocked.

"What are you guys doing here?" Abby looked directly at Delila. "Together?"

"I came over to apologize," Delila told Abby, getting out of the car. "I'm really sorry about the mall. It was totally unfair of me."

"Okay," Abby said. "Thanks. But that still doesn't explain what you're doing here. Together."

Christopher cleared his throat and looked away and Delila flushed. Abby choked on the air in her throat as the realization suddenly hit her like a soccer ball to the head. They weren't just here together. They were *together* together.

"I don't believe it!" Abby said. Her face broke out into a seriously amused grin.

Abby now understood exactly *why* Delila was always asking Abby if she and Christopher were more than friends. And she understood why she had freaked out at the mall—she had been faced with the idea of Christopher and Abby going on a date to the Revolution game—faced with the possibility that Christopher and Abby were finally getting together. Suddenly everything made sense.

Except for the fact that they had always hated each other . . . hadn't they?

"When did this happen?" Abby asked.

Christopher cleared his throat again. "Well, last night we—"

"Um, you guys? I hate to interrupt whatever's going on here, but we're kind of in a totally serious hurry," Carol said, stepping up behind Abby.

Abby looked at her friends and nodded. She really, *really* wanted to hear the story of how and when and why this had all started, but Carol was right. They had to go.

"What's going on?" Christopher asked.

"A lot," Abby replied.

"Oh yeah?" Delila said, raising her eyebrows, intrigued. "Is there anything we can do?"

Abby glanced at Tucker and Carol, who were still hovering by the van, clearly losing patience. She checked her watch. If this wedding was going to happen, Carol and Tucker had to get their butts into their bride-and-groom gear and start acting like a bride and groom. Abby grinned at her friends.

"Yeah," she said. "Actually there is."

• • •

It was a Saturday afternoon and Monique's was bustling with customers, but Abby had no time to lose. She saw the pinched-faced woman who had "helped" her with her dress and wound through the store to catch up with her, Delila trailing behind.

"Excuse me," she said as the woman almost walked past her. "Do you remember me?"

The woman's eyes flicked over Abby and she kept moving. "Sorry, no."

"Hello? Rude much?" Delila said.

Normally Abby would have retreated at this point, giving in to her lifelong habit of avoiding confrontation, but not today. This was too important. This was for her parents. And there was no time to mess around.

"Hey! Annabelle!" she shouted, grabbing the attention of several customers and a few clerks as well. The woman huffed and turned on her heel to look at Abby. "I think you do remember me. You were totally rude to me and my sister a couple of weeks ago when we were in here looking at blue dresses?"

Annabelle's eyes slid toward a haughty-looking woman behind the counter—undoubtedly her manager. The lady shot Annabelle a sour look and Annabelle wisely took a couple of steps toward Abby.

"Is that really necessary?" she whispered.

"Got your attention, didn't it?" Delila said.

"Look, I need the same dress I bought that day, but a size smaller. A six," Abby said. "Do you have one?"

Annabelle sighed and smiled a tight smile for her manager's benefit. "It was the violet blue one, correct?"

"You do remember me!" Abby said with false brightness.

"I'll have to check," Annabelle said, rolling her eyes. "Wait here."

Annabelle turned and hurried away and Delila laughed, tipping her head back.

"Wow!" she said, reaching out to touch Abby's forehead. "Abby? Is that you? Are you feeling okay?"

"Forget that," Abby said, batting her hand away. "What about you? I mean, *Christopher*?"

Delila turned so red she matched her bright red T-shirt. She moved into the corner, away from the crowds, and crossed her arms over her chest.

"You're going to check me into a mental hospital, aren't you?"

"Seriously, Delila, I thought you hated him."

"Sheesh, Ab, don't you know me at all?" Delila said. "I'm always evil to the guys I like. Remember Timothy Desrai?"

Abby raised her eyebrows at the memory. Back in ninth grade, Delila had shown her affection for Timothy by announcing to the entire lunchroom that he had a Cabbage Patch Kid collection in his bedroom closet. She had never been invited to Timothy's house again and ever since, the entire school population had been calling the poor guy CPK.

"You do have kind of a self-destructive streak when it comes to men," Abby said.

"Tell me about it," Delila said, rolling her eyes. "But over the past couple of days Christopher and I have had a couple of real conversations. It started with us talking about you, about how stressed you were about the wedding and how we wished we could help you. But then, last night we actually flirted for a good fifteen minutes outside Häagen-Dazs. We didn't insult each other once."

"You're kidding me," Abby said.

"I know!" Delila replied. "And then he asked me to go to the wedding with him."

"Wow," Abby said. "If it were possible for a person's head to explode from shockedness, that's what my head would be doing right now. Exploding."

"So, think you can handle your two best friends dating?" Delila asked.

"I handled you fighting all the time." Abby gave Delila a giant smile. "This has got to be better, right?"

"Thanks, Ab," Delila said, grabbing her up in a quick hug. "You're the best."

"I know."

Annabelle emerged from the stockroom carrying a violet blue dress in a clear garment bag. She carried it over to Abby and held it up for her, glancing toward her manager.

"Is this the one?" she said.

"Yes, thank you," Abby said, taking the hanger. She glanced at Delila and suddenly got an idea. "Actually, do you have another one in a size two?"

"Oh, no!" Delila said, backing away.

"Well, technically, you did keep a humongous secret from me for months and made my life a living hell forcing me to try and mediate between you two," Abby said. She tilted her head and grinned mischievously. "Did you really think I'd let you get away without punishment?"

"Abby!" Delila exclaimed, her eyes wide and pleading. "I do not do dresses!"

"You do now, Soccerboy-lover," Abby said with a grin.

• • •

"This is so great! I feel like we're in *Charlie's Angels*!" Delila said as she pulled her car back into the Dove's Roost driveway.

"I thought you hated *Charlie's Angels*," Abby said, gripping the top of her door as the wheels tore up the pavement.

"Oh . . . yeah . . . I do," Delila replied. "It just gives me an excuse to drive like a maniac."

"I still can't believe you're with Christopher!" Abby said. "You're such a little vixen!"

"Shut up!" Delila said.

"Delila and Christopher sitting in a tree," Abby sang.

"Shhhhh!" Delila said, spotting Christopher up ahead. She smacked Abby's leg repeatedly until Abby shut up.

Abby smiled. She was so glad to have Delila back. On today of all days, she definitely needed her best friends around. She and Delila pulled up to the top of the drive in time to see Christopher hauling a huge bag out of the back of Abby's van.

"You got it?" Abby called out as Delila slammed on the brakes.

"I think so," Christopher said. He held the bag out across both arms and kicked the back door closed. "I hope it's the right one. I think the woman there thinks I'm wacko."

"Why's that?" Delila asked, pulling the two garment bags out of the back of her car.

"A guy like me asking about a wedding dress?"

Abby laughed and they headed for the house.

"You guys are the best," she said. "I think we may actually pull this off."

Abby's mother was standing around the side of the house. "Bring the dresses up to Carol's room," Abby shouted. "Quick!"

Christopher and Delila disappeared inside just as Abby's mother turned around. "Abigail Lynn Beaumont! Where on earth have you been?" she cried, jogging over in her heels. "The photographer's here and you're not even dressed!"

"I know, Mom. Sorry," Abby said. "I'll go upstairs right now."

"You bet your butt you will," her mother said, shooing her. "Go!"

Abby ran up to her room, laughing all the way. She quickly put on her bridesmaid's dress. Delila helped her fix her hair and put on the bare minimum amount of makeup. She checked herself out in the mirror and grinned.

"You ready for this?" Delila asked.

"So ready," Abby said. "Wish me luck."

"Always," Delila said with a wink.

Abby headed downstairs and out to the yard to join in the picture taking. Tessa and Missy were there in their iridescent plaid. Abby's father, Tucker, Andrew and their dad were all done up in their tuxes, looking very James Bond.

But Carol was the real vision. She looked beautiful. She wore the straight sheath dress she'd loved so much at her fitting with the asymmetrical lace pattern on the skirt. White gloves covered her hands and arms up to her elbows and a veil hung from the top of her bun down her back. Her eyes lit up when Abby walked out and Abby smiled. Her sister was a bride. Well, sort of.

"You look amazing," Abby told her as she joined her in front of the cameras. Carol lifted her bouquet to the side and kissed Abby's cheek as the flashes popped.

"Did you get everything?" Carol whispered.

"We're all set," Abby whispered back.

Together they turned and smiled for the camera, relishing the we-know-something-you-don't-know moment. All around them their parents, aunts and uncles hovered, oohing and ahhing. This was definitely going to be a wedding to remember.

• • •

"Okay, take a deep breath," Abby told Carol. It was T minus thirty minutes to wedding time. They were standing together in the bridal suite at the Dove's Roost, a frilly, flowery room lined with couches. Carol had wisely sent Missy and Tessa off under the pretense that they needed to make sure the aisle runner was straight so that she and Abby would have a chance to do what they needed to do.

"Okay," Carol said. "I'm good."

Abby took a deep breath. "Let's do it."

She opened the door to the bridal suite and looked both ways. Her mother was at one end of the hall, chatting with Liam. Her dad was at the other end going over some things with the justice of the peace. It was time.

"Mom, Dad?" Abby said, practically shaking. "Carol wants to see you guys before she walks down the aisle."

She watched her parents exchange a tentative glance, then they both walked toward her. When the whole family was finally in the same room together, door closed, Abby suddenly started having doubts. The tension in the air was palpable. This room had seen many a last-minute bridal freak-out, many a family squabble, many a total meltdown. It seemed primed for one more. How had they ever thought this was actually going to work?

Her parents were never going to go for it. They were going to explode and make an even bigger scene than they had made at the shower. This had to be the dumbest idea ever.

"Sweetie, you look so beautiful," Abby's mother said, kissing Carol on the cheek.

"Gorgeous," her father added. He checked his watch. "It's almost time to go. What did you want to talk to us about?"

Standing behind her parents, Abby gestured at her sister. This was not right. *Abort mission!* she thought. *Abort mission!*

Carol saw her and shook her head ever so slightly. Somehow, the girl was calm as the bay before a storm. She took a deep breath and looked at her parents. Abby wanted to close her eyes, but somehow she could not make herself do it.

"Mom . . . Dad," Carol said firmly. "I'm not getting married today."

Abby inhaled deeply and then, knowing that there was no going back, that her parents were about to flip out anyway, Abby took her chance, and blurted out the words that had been jamming up her throat for weeks.

"And I got a full scholarship to study in Italy next year," she said. "I'm going to Italy!"

· 16 ·

Sacred Vows

"What on earth do you mean, you're not getting married!" Abby's mother screeched.

"Italy! Who says you're going to Italy?" her father shouted, red in the face.

"Dad, just let me explain," Abby said. She was glad that her parents had two pieces of news to deal with and weren't ganging up on her together. "Remember, like, months ago I told you about that exchange program Delila was doing and you said you didn't have the money to send me?"

"Yes, I recall," her father said. Carol and her mom

were talking too, but Abby had to tune them out to pay attention to her father. "Did you win the lottery since then?"

"No. But I did find out that they have scholarships for this thing. *And* that Roberto Viola, only the most amazing soccer player in history, is going to be coaching there," Abby said. "So I applied just to see what would happen and I got in! With a full scholarship."

"So you've already applied and gotten funding. I'm sorry, when, exactly, were you planning on telling your mother and me about your plans to spend a year in a foreign country? Were you going to write us a postcard once you already got there?"

"Well, you guys haven't exactly been the easiest people to talk to lately," Abby shot back, her defense mechanism kicking in.

"Just because your mother and I are having problems, that's no excuse for you to keep secrets from us," her father said. "Especially not ones as big as this!"

"It's not like I don't already feel guilty about this!" Abby replied. "It's not like I didn't *want* to tell you—you've just been too preoccupied tearing each other apart!"

Her father's face fell and Abby felt a pang in her heart. Had she said too much? Gone too far? Either way, the break in their argument left only one voice in the room—her mother's.

"But all those people . . . ," Abby's mother was saying. Her mother sat down on the divan, her face pale and her hands shaky. She reached out to grasp Abby's hand. "What're we going to tell all those people?"

"You're going to tell them that they're still going to get to see a wedding," Abby said. She sat down at her mother's side.

"What? Please don't tell me you and Noah Spencer are eloping," Abby's father said.

"Noah Spencer?" Her mother sounded even more confused. "Are you dating Noah Spencer?"

"Yeah . . . no . . . um, kind of?" Abby said. "Maybe not." She brought her hands to her head and looked at Carol. "A little help here?"

"Abby is not eloping," Carol said. "She came up with this plan and if you guys agree, we both think it would be really cool."

"Will somebody please tell me who is supposed to be getting married here?" Abby's father demanded.

"You and Mom!" Abby blurted out. "Carol and I want you to renew your vows."

Total silence ensued. Abby's mom looked at her dad and they held each other's gaze for a split second before her father looked away.

"Girls . . . while that's a very sweet gesture . . . I really don't think this is the time," Abby's mother said.

"Have either of you guys even seen the ballroom today?" Carol asked.

Abby's parents spoke at once.

"I haven't actually had time—"

"No, not since it was finished—"

Abby smiled. "Come on," she said. "We want to show you something."

Abby and Carol led their parents down the hallway and into the lounge, then through the double doors into the ballroom. Even though she'd seen it all before, the sight was still breathtaking to Abby. She had never seen the room look so beautiful.

"Oh my goodness!" Abby's mother gasped, her hand over her heart.

Her dad was so shocked, he could only add, "Wow."

They stepped to the center of the room, each of them turning around in the middle of the dance floor to take it all in. The beautiful array of colors, the crystal twinkling in the waning sunlight, the ribbons and flowers and candles. Over the years Abby's parents had seen it all, but this was something new. Abby exchanged a triumphant glance with Carol. It was all coming together.

"You guys did this together," Abby told her parents. "You didn't even realize you were doing it. But, I mean . . . look at it."

"You thought your two styles were completely different, but when they came together they made this," Carol added. "It's the most gorgeous wedding I've ever seen."

Abby's parents looked at each other and her mother smiled softly. And Abby could swear she saw tears in her father's eyes. She took a few steps toward them.

"I don't know if I'm right, but I think that you were each trying to plan the wedding you never had," Abby told them softly. "I mean, how insane is it that two such wedding-obsessed people eloped? You guys never got to do it up the way you wanted, so you were trying to do it for Carol. That's why I think you should have your own wedding, today, the way each of you always wanted."

"So? What do you think?" Carol asked.

"The flowers really are beautiful, Phoebe," Abby's father said.

"And the colors . . . ," her mom said. "The colors are amazing, David."

"Abby's right," her dad said. "I think we were both using Carol to throw our own dream weddings."

Abby's mother looked sheepishly at the floor. "I'm the horrendous mother of the bride to end all horrendous mothers of the bride, aren't I?"

"Mom, no!" Carol said, stepping forward to hug her. "I appreciate everything you tried to do." She leaned back and looked at both of them. "But if you do it again when I really get married, you are so dead."

All four of them laughed and Abby's entire body relaxed. It was as if the last couple of months were being washed away.

"So, what do you think, David?" Abby's mother said. "Wanna get hitched?"

Her father stepped forward, broke into a grin and took Abby's mother's hand. "Phoebe Beaumont, will you marry me?"

Abby and Carol grinned. They high-fived into a hug as their parents kissed.

"Christopher! Let's go!" Abby shouted.

Christopher walked in from the hall, smiled at Abby's parents and strode right past them out the back door.

"All right, people," he shouted to the crowd. "We have a small change of plans here. . . ."

"Dad, you wait at the arch," Abby said. "We've got to get the bride ready."

Her mother giggled as Abby and Carol dragged her upstairs to Carol's room. When they opened the door, Delila was already decked out in her bridesmaid's dress. The gown her mother had loved back at the bridal shop hung on the closet door in all its lacy, beaded glory. Her mother's mouth dropped open when she saw it.

"Oh, girls . . . ," she said. She walked over to touch the fabric gently.

"You're going to look just like a princess," Carol told her. "Just like you always wanted."

The Wedding Ceremony

Of

Phoebe Larissa Beaumont
~~Carol Marie Beaumont~~

And
~~And~~

David Jonathan Beaumont
~~Tucker Clint Robb~~

Officiant: Justice Randolph Markenson

Maid of Honor: Abigail Lynn Beaumont
And Carol Marie Beaumont
Bridesmaids: Tessa Leone, Missy Marx
and Delila Barber

Tucker Robb
Best Man: ~~Andrew Robb~~

"And now, as I understand it, David and Phoebe have written their own vows that they would like to share with each other," the justice of the peace said with a smile.

Abby glanced at Carol, who stood alongside her in her blue bridesmaid's dress with Tessa, Missy and Delila. When had this vow thing been decided? And how had her parents had the time to think up something to say? Abby's dad took both her mother's hands in his own and swallowed hard.

"Phoebe, when we first got married we were just a couple of crazy kids with a dream," he said, causing her mother to laugh and tear up at the same time. "We dreamt of being together. We dreamt of having a family. We dreamt of having a business. And now . . . look around us," he said, glancing up at the Dove's Roost and at Abby and Carol. "We have everything we always wanted and more. How many people can say that they truly love what they do? How many people can say that they have daughters who know them even better than they know themselves?"

Both Abby's parents looked at her and Carol again and tears stung at Abby's eyes. What was her father *doing* to her?

"I know how lucky we are, Phoebe. But most of all I know how lucky I am to have you. And so, on this day, I promise to love you always. To cherish you forever. And to remember every day what an honor it is to be a part of your family."

Someone in the back started a round of applause and Abby shoved her flowers under her arm and joined in, the tears overflowing. Abby's mother threw her arms around her father and hugged him.

"He took what I was going to say!" she shouted, laughing through her tears.

Everyone cracked up and it was one of the more cathartic moments of Abby's life. She felt as if every emotion she'd felt over the past few months were draining out of her. She saw Carol and Tucker exchange a long, meaningful glance. Abby knew what they were thinking—that the two of them were going to exchange vows one day, too. The thought actually made Abby happy.

She couldn't believe how quickly everything had changed. Three days before she had been certain that Tucker was cheating on her sister. Three days before her parents had been embroiled in a silent war. Three days before she was barely speaking to her best friend. Now, with the sun shining down on her, warming her shoulders and face, with practically everyone she knew cheering and blowing bubbles around her, Abby knew that everything was going to be okay. Her parents would work out their problems, and she could handle Tucker being part of her life. She could even handle Delila and Christopher dating—as long as they didn't get all gross and mushy on her.

While the justice of the peace delivered his wrap-up speech, Abby looked around. The aisle was beautifully decorated with light blue and white ribbons. The arch was gorgeous, covered in blue, white and yellow flowers. Everyone looked absolutely beautiful. Abby took a deep breath and let it out slowly. She couldn't believe she had pulled it off. It seemed she had actually become a wedding guru after all. Well, with Becky, Carol, Christopher and Delila's help.

"By the power vested in me by the state of Massachusetts, I now pronounce you man and wife . . . again!" the justice announced.

Everyone applauded again as Abby's parents kissed, no one clapping harder than Abby herself. It was one of those ideal moments. One of those rare blips in time where everything was totally perfect.

But even as Abby realized this, her heart twisted in her chest, reminding her that, in fact, all was not well. There was one thing missing. Clutching her bouquet, she turned to follow her parents up the aisle and saw him. Not missing after all. Noah Spencer was standing at the back of the ceremony area, his blue eyes focused directly on her.

· 17 ·

Always a Bridesmaid

*A*bby swallowed back her fear and walked toward Noah. The rest of the guests were walking toward the cocktail hour on the flagstone patio behind the house.

"Hey," she said quietly. Abby was so nervous she could barely look at Noah. She tried to concentrate on her bouquet.

"Hey," he replied. "Sorry to crash. I felt guilty about sending the new guy over with the cake this morning and I wanted to make sure it all turned out okay."

"Right. Well, it did. Thanks," Abby said, forcing a smile.

"Johnny Rockets told me what you did for your parents," Noah said. "I wanted to tell you I think it's totally amazing."

"Glad you think so," Abby replied. Then she took a deep breath.

"Listen, about Italy," she said. "I didn't tell you because I wasn't even sure I was going to be allowed to go. And I didn't want to, you know, complicate everything. We were just getting together. We'd just said . . ."

The words died in her throat, choking her up. There was no way she was getting them out in the middle of all this.

"I love you?" Noah supplied.

Abby looked up and it was as if his eyes were burning a hole in her heart. Did he still love her, or had it fizzled faster than it had started?

"Look, I'm sorry for overreacting," Noah said finally. "I just didn't want to lose you, and the Italy thing combined with the Johnny Rockets thing . . . I don't know, I guess I was threatened and somehow that made me regress back to kindergarten."

Abby snorted a laugh, then covered her mouth with her hand. She had never heard a guy admit so much in one sentence.

"She laughs. I take that as a good sign," Noah said.

"Everything's been so crazy for so long," Abby said. "Do you think maybe we could just . . ."

"Start over?" Noah supplied.

"Yeah," Abby said hopefully.

"Sounds like a plan," Noah said. He reached out and took her free hand and that was all Abby needed to complete her day. She was utterly happy.

"Do you want to go get something to eat?" Abby asked. "I'm starved."

Noah smiled, understanding that all was well between them. "Absolutely."

They walked up to the patio together. Guests were mingling and snacking on finger foods. There were small tables draped in white linen tablecloths with small flower arrangements at the center. Every available pole, gutter and grate was covered in ribbons that were fluttering in the breeze. Rocco carved turkey and roast beef at the meat and cheese station while Big Pete served up fresh lobster and shrimp at the seafood station. Little Pete cleared used plates and napkins. Glasses clinked and silverware chimed. Becky stood back in the corner, watching it all with a satisfied smile. Abby felt as light as air. It was time to finally relax.

"Abby!" her mother said, practically skipping over to her. Her mother wrapped her up in a huge bear hug, clutching her so hard Abby could feel the beads of the wedding gown pressing into her skin. "Thank you so much for this day. I don't know what your father and I have been thinking, but this was exactly what we needed."

"Exactly," her father said, joining them. He handed his wife a glass of champagne and took a sip from his own. "We're sorry about everything you've been through the last few months. You must have hated us."

"I never hated you, Dad," Abby said. "I was just worried."

"Well, your father and I just talked about it, and we need to look over the paperwork for this exchange program. But if it all checks out, well then, you can go."

"We'll miss you, of course, but we know we can't keep you here forever," her dad added.

"You only live once, Abby," her mother said. "You gave us a second chance at our wedding tonight, but you may never get an opportunity like this again."

Abby felt as if she were about to overflow with emotion. She was going to Italy! Her parents had said yes!

All the muscles in Noah's face went slack.

"Noah, the cake looks beautiful," Abby's mother said as her parents started to move away. "We need to say hello to a few more people, but we'll talk about this more later." She squeezed Abby's hand before heading off to say hello to Abby's aunt.

Abby's father pinched her cheek quickly and followed his wife, leaving Abby alone to deal with her sort-of boyfriend.

"So, that's great that they said yes," Noah said, pushing his hands into his pockets.

"Yeah . . . ," Abby said slowly.

"Do you think you'll go?" Noah asked.

"Yeah, I think I will," Abby replied. "My parents are right, Noah. I have to do this. If there's one thing I can take from all this—Carol and Tucker and my parents—it's that you have to do what you have to do, you know? If I don't go to Italy, it'll be for you . . . and I'll just end up resenting it later."

"Resenting me," Noah said, looking at the ground.

"I'm sorry," Abby said, tears stinging at her eyes. "I know the timing sucks. Believe me, I know."

"It's okay," Noah said, raising his head to look her in the eye. "I understand. I really do." He reached out for her hand and she laced her fingers through his again. "I'm just really going to miss you."

"I'm going to miss you too."

At that moment, the doors to the ballroom opened and the crowd hushed slightly. Abby looked up to see Becky, totally in her element, raise her hands in the air, palms up. "Everyone please join us in the ballroom!" she announced with her perfect smile. "It's time to party!"

• • •

Abby stood at the edge of the dance floor between Noah and Carol. Standing behind Carol was Tucker, who had his arms wrapped around her. In the center of the floor, with candles twinkling all around, her parents waltzed to the theme from *Sleeping Beauty,* one of Abby's mother's favorite movies. As she watched her parents gaze into each other's eyes, she could almost imagine what they might have looked like on their first wedding day twenty-three years before.

"Wow, Abby. You almost look moved," Carol said, nudging her with her elbow.

"Me? Nah," Abby said, waving her hand. "I was just thinking about the scene all the guests are gonna make when they find out we have carrot cake."

Carol clucked her tongue and rolled her eyes. "You try to do something original and this one's all over you. You know, Abby. I'm beginning to think you're more of a traditionalist than you like to admit."

Abby's jaw dropped, but she never got a chance to protest. Roger Birnbaum, the leader of her parents' favorite band, Twilight, came to the microphone. He was decked out in a black tuxedo as always, his silver hair practically glowing in the candlelight.

"And now our bride and groom would like their daughters and their dates to join them on the dance floor!" he announced.

Noah took Abby's hand and pulled her out from the crowd. "I've been waiting for this all night," he said, pulling her into his arms.

Abby laughed as Carol and Tucker twirled by, doing an exaggerated waltz. Everyone applauded and sniffled and looked truly moved. Abby had to bury her face in Noah's shoulder to keep from overdosing on the cheesiness of the moment. Here was one more thing she had never done before—danced in front of a weepy crowd.

"So . . . Italy, huh?" Noah squeezed the fingers of her right hand as they moved in a slow circle.

Abby's heart gave a nervous and sad pang. Was she going to feel like this every time the subject came up? Excited but melancholy all at once?

"Yeah," she said, looking up at him. "It's kinda far away, isn't it?"

Noah tilted his head. "I don't know. Maybe it won't be so bad."

"Oh, really?" she asked. "Have you moved on already?"

The last few strains of the song filled the room and Noah stopped moving. He put his hands on Abby's waist and leaned in close to her.

"Actually, I understand Italy has some killer schools for the pastry and baking arts," he whispered in her ear just as the song came to a close.

Abby felt a shiver all down her spine. She looked up into Noah's eyes as everyone on the dance floor applauded the Beaumont family.

"What about your dad? I thought you needed to be here for him," Abby said as all the other guests ran out onto the dance floor. Predictably ignoring Abby's do-not-play list, Twilight launched into a raucous version of "Celebration" and the whole room started to shake around them.

"We can always hire an interim decorator," Noah shouted over the music. "We'll have to interview about a thousand people, but still. I'm sure my dad would agree with the whole 'You only live once' thing."

"So you're serious," Abby said in happy disbelief. "You want to come to Italy."

"Yeah! I can hone my craft and be with you," Noah said with a grin. "I kind of see that as a win-win. What do you think?"

"I think . . . ," Abby said, throwing one arm around his neck, then the other. "I think that this Italy trip just got a whole lot more appealing."

Noah reached up and ran his fingers along her cheek. "*Ti amo*, Abby."

Abby laughed. "What does *that* mean?"

"It means 'I love you'!" Noah exclaimed. "Jeez! Haven't you been studying?"

"You are so cheesy!" she replied, shoving his shoulder. "You learned to say 'I love you' in Italian?"

"All right, that's it. I'm outta here!" Noah said, throwing his hands up.

Abby grabbed him around the waist before he could get away and pulled him to her, laughing.

"C'mere, loser," she said.

He smiled, his lips hovering ever so close to hers. "Freakshow," he said softly.

Then Abby kissed him, right there in the center of the party, with a hundred Kool-and-the-Gang-crazed guests jumping up and down around them. Her parents were wrapped up in their just-married daze, her sister and Tucker were giggling over glasses of champagne, Delila and Christopher were dancing together, laughing and looking for all the world like they had never said an unkind word to each other.

Somehow, the Dove's Roost Chateau had worked its magic on her family and friends. As she stood in the middle of the dance floor Abby realized, for the first time, that not every wedding had to be a dish-tossing disaster. And maybe, just maybe, there was such a thing as a happy ending.

Dear Mom, Dad and Carol,

Buon giorno! We're all having a great time in Venice (Venezia). No one's killed each other yet, but Christopher threatened to drown himself in one of the canals yesterday (ieri) if Delila and I didn't stop trying to sing TV show themes in Italian. (The Brady Bunch sounds really cool!) Noah got his master baker's certificate on Friday (venerdi) and plans to make us all fat (grasso) before we get home. Hope all is going well at the Roost! Love to you and to Tucker as well.

Abby

Win a Shopping Spree!

You had to wear an ugly dress— now you deserve a reward!

When Abby's sister announces that she is getting married, Abby is forced to step in as maid of honor. So what if the dress is dreadful? Abby can handle it. After all, it's just one day. Right?

Bridesmaids are always destined to wear hideous dresses. What is the worst dress you ever wore? Send in a picture of yourself in your ugliest dress and tell us in 100 words or less why you had to wear it.

One grand-prize winner will receive a $500 gift certificate from their favorite store.

All entries must be received by September 1, 2005.

Enter now!

Visit www.randomhouse.com/teens/bridesmaid for complete rules and details.

Delacorte
Press

RANDOM HOUSE
CHILDREN'S BOOKS